When the Time Comes

When the Time Comes

Maurice Blanchot

translated
by
Lydia Davis

STATION
HILL

Originally published in French under the title *Au Moment voulu*, copyright © 1951 by Editions Gallimard.

First edition.

Published by Station Hill Press, Barrytown, New York 12507, with partial support from the New York State Council on the Arts and the National Endowment for the Arts.

Produced by the Open Studio Typesetting & Design Project, Barrytown, New York, funded in part by the New York State Council on the Arts and the National Endowment for the Arts.

Designed by Susan Quasha.

Library of Congress Cataloging in Publication Data

Blanchot, Maurice.
    When the time comes.

    Translation of: Au moment voulu.
    I. Title.
PQ2603.L3343A913 1985   843'.912   84-12373
ISBN 0-930794-96-6
ISBN 0-930794-95-8 (pbk.)

Manufactured in the United States of America.

Translator's Note

Like other works of Maurice Blanchot, this novel is rife with syntactical and semantic difficulties. Often, however, in translating his work, to clarify is to simplify and to betray. The challenge for the translator, then, is to write the book in English with an equivalent of Blanchot's limpid obscurity.

I would like to thank P. Adams Sitney and Paul Auster for taking the time to read over this translation and point out the moments when the prose became either too limpid or too obscure.

Because the friend who lived with her was not there, the door was opened by Judith. I was extremely, inextricably surprised, certainly much more so than if I had met her by chance. My astonishment was such that it expressed itself in me with these words: "God! Still a face I know!" (Maybe my decision to walk right up to this face had been so strong that it made the face impossible.) But there was also the embarrassment of having come to confirm, here and now, the continuity of things. Time had passed, and yet it was not past; that was a truth that I should not have wanted to place in my presence.

I don't know if the surprise felt by this face was the same as mine. Yet there was clearly such an accumulation of events between us, excessive things, torments, incredible thoughts and also such a depth of happy forgetfulness that it was not at all hard for her not to be surprised by me. I found her surprisingly little changed. The small rooms had been transformed, as I saw right away, but even in this new setting, which I was not managing to take in yet and which I didn't like very much, she was completely the same, not only faithful to her features, to her appearance, but also to her age—young in a way that made her strangely resemble herself. I kept looking at her, I said to myself: So this is why I was so surprised. Her face, or rather her expression, which hardly varied at all, remaining halfway between a most cheerful smile and a most chilly reserve, reawakened in me a terribly distant memory, and it was this

1

deeply buried, very ancient memory that she seemed to be copying in order to appear so young. At last I said to her: "You really have changed very little!" At this moment she was next to a piano I had never imagined in that room. Why this piano? "Are you the one who plays the piano?" She shook her head. Quite a long time afterwards, with sudden animation and in a reproachful tone of voice, she said to me: "Claudia's the one who plays! She sings!" She was looking at me in a strange, spontaneous, lively way, and yet out of the corner of her eye. This look—I don't know why—struck me to the very quick. "Who is Claudia?" She did not answer, and again I was struck, but this time so much so, as though by some misfortune, that I became uneasy about the look of resemblance she had, which made her so absolutely young. Now I remembered her much better. She had the most delicate sort of face, I mean that her features had a sort of playfulness and extreme fragility, as though they were controlled by a different appearance, one that was more concentrated, interior, as though age could only harden them. But that was just what had not happened, age had been strangely reduced to impotence. After all, why should she have changed? The past was not so far back, it couldn't be such a great misfortune either. And even I—how could I deny it?—now that I could look at her from the depths of my memory, I was uplifted, taken back to another life. Yes, a strange impulse came to me, an unforgotten possibility that cared nothing for the days, that shone out through the darkest night, a blind force against which surprise and grief could do nothing.

The window was open, and she got up to go and shut it. I realized that until then the street had continued to run through the room. I don't know if all that noise bothered her; I think she wasn't paying much attention to it; but when she turned around and saw me I had the sudden feeling that only then was she seeing me for the first time. I admit that this was a remarkable

2

thing, and at the same moment I also felt—still in an unclear way but already acutely—that it was partly my fault: yes, I saw right away that if in some sense I had escaped her notice—and that was perhaps odd—I had also not done everything I should have done in order really to let her catch sight of me, and it was much less odd than it was saddening. For one reason or another, but maybe because I myself had been too busy watching her quite confortably, something essential that could only happen if I asked it to happen had been forgotten, and for the moment I didn't know what it was, but forgetfulness was as present as it could be, so much so, especially now that the room was shut up, as to allow me to suspect that outside of it there wasn't much here.

This was, I must say, a discovery so disastrous physically that it took complete control of me. As I was thinking that, I was fascinated by my thought, and overshadowed by it. Well, it was an idea! And not just any idea but one that was proportional to me, exactly equal to me, and if it allowed itself to be thought, I had to disappear. After a moment I had to ask for a glass of water. The words "Give me a glass of water" left me with a feeling of terrible coldness. I was in pain, but completely myself again, and more particularly I had no doubt about what had just happened. When I made up my mind to extricate myself, I tried to remember where the kitchen was. In the hallway it was strangely dark, and I realized because of this that I still wasn't very well. On one side there was the bathroom that opened into the room I had just left, and the kitchen and the second room had to be farther on: in my mind everything was clear, but not outside. Blasted hallway, I thought, was it really this long? Now, when I think of how I was behaving, I'm surprised that I could have made all those efforts without realizing why they cost me so much. I'm not sure I even felt anything unpleasant until the point when, after an awkward movement (having perhaps bumped into a wall), I experienced an atrocious pain, the most lively pain possible—it split my head open—but perhaps more lively than alive; it is hard to express how it was at once cruel and insignificant: a horrible violence, an atrocity, all the more intolerable because it seemed to come to me across a fantastic layer of time, burning in its entirety inside me, an immense and unique pain, as though I had not been touched at this moment but centuries ago and for centuries past, and the quality it had of being something finished, something completely dead, could certainly make it easier to bear but also harder, by turning it into a perseverance that was absolutely cold, impersonal, that would not be stopped either by life or by the end of life. Of course I did not fathom all that right away. I was simply penetrated by a feeling of horror, and by these words, which I still believe: "Oh no, is this beginning again? Again! Again!" I was stopped short, in any case. Wherever it came from, the shock had overtaken me so vigorously that there was enough room in the present instant which it opened up for me to forget endlessly to emerge from it. Walk, go forward—I could certainly do that, and I had to, but rather like an ox that has been hit over the head: my steps were the steps of immobility. These were the most difficult moments. And it is really true that they still endure; through everything, I must turn back to them, and say to myself: I'm still there, I stayed there.

The hallway led to the room that was at the other end. Everything seems to indicate that I looked terribly distraught, I went in more or less without knowing it, without any feeling of going from one place to another, filled with a motionless falling, I couldn't see, I was miles from realizing I couldn't see. I probably stopped on the doorsill. After all, there was a passage there, a thickness that had its own laws or requirements. Finally—finally?—the passage became free, I forced the entrance, and I took two or three steps into the room. Fortunately (but maybe

4

this impression was accurate only for me), I walked with a certain discretion. Fortunately too, as soon as I was really inside a little of that reality touched me. The afternoon, in the meantime, had taken a large leap forward, but there was just enough light so that I could tolerate it. At least I had the feeling I could, just as I recognized in the calm, the patience, and the very weakness of the daylight a concern to respect the life in me that was still so weak. What I did not see, what I saw only at the last... but I would like to be able to pass over all that quickly. I often have an immeasurable desire to abbreviate, a desire that is powerless, because to satisfy it would be too easy for me; however lively it might be, it is too weak for the limitless power I have to accomplish it. Oh, how useless it is to desire anything.

As for this young woman who had opened the door for me, to whom I had talked, who had been real enough, from the past to the present, during an inestimable length of time, to remain constantly visible to me—I would like to let nothing be understood about her, ever. My need to name her, to make her appear in circumstances which, however mysterious they may be, are still those of living people, has a violence about it that horrifies me. This is the reason for my desire to abbreviate, at least its nobler aspect. To pass over the essential—that is what the essential asks of me, asks of me through this desire. If it is possible, let it be this way. I beg my decline to come by itself.

I saw certain parts of the room very clearly, and it had already renewed its alliance with me, but I didn't see her. I don't know why. Soon I looked with interest at a large armchair placed at the far end of the bed (so I had taken several steps into the room in order to reach the foot of the bed); in a corner near the window I noticed a little table with a pretty mirror, but the word for this piece of furniture didn't come to me. At that instant I was near the window, I felt almost well, and if it was true that the daylight was waning as fast as it was mounting again in me, what lucidity remained here and there was enough to show me everything without illusion. I can even say that if I was a little disoriented in that room, that disorientation would have been natural during any visit to anybody, in any one of the thousand rooms I could have gone into.

The only vestige of anomaly was that although no one was there—or I saw no one—this didn't in the least disturb the feeling of naturalness. As far as I know, I found the situation perfect, I didn't want to see the door open and the man or woman who normally lived there come in. In fact, I didn't imagine that anyone lived in the room, or in any other room in the world, if there were any others, which didn't occur to me either. I think for me, at that moment, the world was fully represented by this room with its bed in the middle of it, the armchair and its little piece of furniture. Really, where could anyone have come from? It would have been madness to expect the walls to disappear. Besides, I was not conscious of the world.

Well, according to what she told me, she saw me; she was actually standing in front of the armchair and not one of my movements had escaped her. It was true, I had remained next to the door for quite a few minutes, but not at all with that horribly distraught look I thought I had; rather pale, yes, and with an expression that was cold, "fixed," she said, which made it very clear—but this was a little troubling, even so—that my life was taking place somewhere else and that there could be nothing of me there but this endless immobility. It was also true that I had taken a few steps; passing near the armchair, I had gone to the little piece of furniture and looked at it with interest, I was visibly interested in it, in some sense it served as the justification for my having come in. No, she wasn't surprised to see me paying so little attention to the fact that she was present— because at such a moment she wasn't at all anxious, either, to know if she was present, because even though being cast into the

6

shadow involves some sacrifices, she also took infinite satisfaction in watching me in my truthfulness, for I, not seeing her and not seeing anyone, showed myself in all the sincerity of a man who is alone. To contemplate the truth in flesh and blood, even if one must remain invisible, even if one must plunge forever into the discretion of the most desperate cold and the most radical separation — who hasn't wanted that? But who has had that courage? Only one person, I think.

Why didn't I see her? As I said, I don't really know. It's hard to go back over an impossible thing when it has been surmounted, even harder when one isn't sure the impossibility isn't still there. Countless men walk by one another and never meet; no one thinks this is scandalous; who would want to be seen by everyone? But perhaps I was still everyone, perhaps I was the great number and the inexhaustible multitude — who can say? For me this room was the world, and for my little strength and my little interest it had the immensity of the world; who would require a look to cross the universe? What is strange about not seeing something distant when nearby things are still invisible? Yes, what is inexplicable is not my ignorance but the fact that my ignorance gave in. I would find it unfair, though in keeping with the laws, not to have been able to shatter infinity, nor draw from all the hazards the only one that could be called chance. Bitter chance, and heaped with misfortune, but no matter — chance! Well, I had it, and even if it is lost, I still have it, I'll have it forever. This is what should be surprising.

Things appeared to resolve themselves (appeared? that was already a great deal). At the moment I was closest to her, two steps from the armchair, she could not only see me better, my face livid rather than pale, my forehead cruelly swollen, but almost touch me. This feeling of having brushed against me seemed very strange to her and drove away all other reflections: this was something unexpected, even more, a light that she hadn't glimpsed a second before. After that she followed me with different eyes. Did I exist, then? Then perhaps I existed for her too! Life, she said to herself, and suddenly she had the strength, the immense strength to cry out at me, and while I leaned over the objects on the dresser, she actually did utter a cry that seemed to her to be born, to leap out, from the living memory of her name, but — why? — valiant though this cry was, it did not go beyond its boundaries, it did not reach me, and because of that, she herself did not hear it. Maybe she resigned herself to this. As the daylight faded very fast, she saw less and less of what was happening in the room. Of course it was a room, but all the same so little a room; and certainty could not reside within four walls. What certainty? She did not know, something that resembled her and made her resemble the cold and tranquillity of transparent things.

Pride also! The wild statement that has no rights, the pact signed with what defies the origin, oh strange and terrible tranquillity. She went mysteriously past, at one remove from the visible lies, more obvious than she could possibly have been, and the terror she must really have felt at getting lost and always starting to get lost again in the unlimited obviousness had apparently not been more remote than the simple fear of a little girl encountering the dark, late one afternoon, in a garden. Life, she repeated to herself, but already this word was no longer being spoken by anyone, was in no way addressed to me. Life was now a sort of bet being conceived nearby, a bet with the memory of that touch — had it happened? — with that stupefying feeling — would it persist? — that not only did not fade but asserted itself — it too — in the wild manner of something that could have no end, that would always make claims, make demands, that had already set itself in motion, wandered and wandered like a blind thing, without any goal and yet more and more greedy, incapable of seeking anything but turning faster and faster in a furious vertigo, without any voice, walled up, a desire, a shiver turned to stone. It may be that I had a presentiment of this (but hadn't I had this presentiment much earlier? Without it would I have gone in?). That she then rose up before me, not as an empty illusion, but as the imminence of a monumental storm, as the infinite thickness of a breath of granite precipitated against my forehead, yes, but this shock was not a new truth either, nor was the cry that came to me new, nor was the one I heard new, only the immense surprise of the calm was new, an abrupt silence that brought everything to a stop. This caused a remarkable gap, but what did it mean: was it the repose after annihilation? The glory of the next to the last day? I hardly had time to ask myself that, just barely time to seize the truth of that touch—I too—take it by surprise and say to her: "What! You were here! Now!"

Claudia came back shortly afterwards. I didn't know her. As I could see, she was a resolute person who wasn't easily swayed, the same age, I think, as Judith, and her friend since childhood, but who backed her up more like an older sister with a strong character. She had no lack of talents. She had performed brilliantly in the theater, the sort of theater where people sang, and she really did have a voice that could be called very beautiful, dazzling and yet austere, an unforgiving voice. I suppose she knew more about me than most of the people who had come close to me. I imagine that in the beginning Judith had talked to her about me: very little, but endlessly, even so—that was the gloomy side of things. (I had said to her: "I want to live in darkness." But the truth spoke in her without her knowing it, and even when she said nothing, she was still speaking; behind her wall, she was asserting something.)

So I have to think that she was expecting me to return. At least, if she remained disconcerted when she saw me—and I'm sure that she drew back, that for an instant she tried to go back the way she had come, as though, confronted with my presence, she had attempted to find a way out that would have given her the possibility of having been there before me, of having been in a position to open the door for me herself and greet me in her own way—yes, I believe this motion of drawing back was an attempt to recapture her absence, and the effect of it for me, which I blindly took advantage of, was to create a refuge for me in my own amazement and my agitation, which was immense—when she appeared, perhaps I was holding the outcome in my hands and then everything was called into question again. Actually, within my distress, I felt a sort of admiration for the way she went about avoiding total shipwreck. Certainly composure was one of her qualities, and not simply presence of mind but a correct feeling for what had to be known and not known, kept and abandoned. Perhaps, when she saw me, when she recognized me, even as she blunted the edge of the first instant with a skill that had to be attributed to her self-control but which was undoubtedly also the backflow of the movement that had carried me forward—perhaps, driven by her fighting instinct, she said to herself: "Now I won't ever let him go again." I have to admit that the promptness with which she contrived to cut off my retreat gave me this impression. It seems to me she seized upon precisely the point from which it was hardly possible for me to do anything else but what she might choose to decide. I could have seen to it that I was taken elsewhere, I could have appealed to someone else? That's true, and I didn't do it. But did I want to leave? I'm not even convinced that she believed I was seriously ill; it was more that the appearance of the illness became the language that allowed her to speak, the guarantee that entitled her to act in a natural way. I really have to admire the way she was able to think alone, the way she remained free and fought actively, with all the resources of a sleepless attention—and did I fight? Can it be called a fight? Not against her, anyway; at a moment like that, I could not carry her

10

into the center of myself, which belonged to someone else: she lived in the outskirts, at the limit, where difficulties turn into active and real things. This doesn't mean that she was without importance. On the contrary, she whispered at me from that borderland where she was free, she whispered preoccupations that paralyzed time. This paralysis was her victory, this inertia became my struggle.

With her ability to organize quickly — actually, perhaps not all that quickly: quick only next to the slowness of the rest of us — she hurried to settle me on a couch across from the piano. She seemed to be impelled by a strange idea — but perhaps it was pure passion, the pure desire to remain the only one in charge of this place — by the need to snatch me from the room as fast as possible. To keep me, but first to keep me out of here. (Naturally — it was their room, nothing could be more normal than such an arrangement; but her haste? her feverishness as long as I wasn't leaving?)

No less striking was the fact that once she had settled me in the studio she didn't leave me there alone but shut us up there together, I mean she went away immediately with a reserve, a discretion, that may have meant she would not impose herself, but which also had another meaning that I understood very well, without being able to pin it down exactly. To give some idea what it was, I could say that the only aspect of the apartment that made it seem roomy was the hallway that divided it into two areas, but at certain moments she turned it into an immense, desert space, in which it seemed not that we were alone, but, what was much more impressive, that she was alone, that she alone was real, that she alone was endowed with the opulence and the perseverance of life. And, at the same time, this reserve seemed to create a special bond between us, as though, in order to confirm an allusion contained or expressed by my presence, she had given me to understand that where she was concerned I didn't have to worry, she wouldn't say one word more than she should.

If I go back over this instant, the first instant in which, because of that reserve, we were in one another's presence again, but this time cruelly trapped facing each other, I feel as though I am in some way bound to a sadness, and an anxiety, that are capable of obscuring everything. After a short time, probably because she was alone with me—she was there, like a sort of image, made possible by the course of things and the good will of the daily order—I saw that she was feeling embarrassed, uneasy, and that she was also moved by a slight, unstable impulse, a cold gaity that made her difficult to grasp: this showed in her breathing, which wasn't as tranquil as it had been, and in her glance, where a rather strange sparkling glimmer shone like the reflection of a distant resentment, and at last her face assumed an expression of astonishment, of questioning. I hadn't the least notion of how deep that look was. I myself was as weak as I could be, and to say that I showed no understanding wouldn't be saying very much: I wasn't able to read her eyes. I was turning back bitterly towards that meeting a hair's breadth from the end, when the alien power had won out, and this sort of memory couldn't make me feel happy again right away. I said to her—I repeated several times rather sharply: "What's the matter with you? Tell me what's the matter!" When the light was out, I recalled this "What's the matter?", and it horrified me. It was a false cry, a clumsy question imbued with a suspicion, a cold, disconcerting thought. After that, she certainly would have been at a loss to know if "something was the matter" with her. But by way of this suspicion it seems to me that I returned to myself, a solitary self, distant and scattered, retreating before time, who didn't say "you" to anyone in an intimate way and in the presence of whom no one could say "me". I realized it was a strange suspicion, the most confusing kind of illusion, and this confusion didn't reflect the infinite vision of perspectives opening one onto the next, but the sterile sadness of chaos, the afflicted uncertainty that closes itself up again and withdraws, shaking itself.

I got up immediately, determined not to let this cry move across the night. I didn't make much noise. Nevertheless, at the other end of the hallway Claudia was already watching me come near. This was really our first contact; until then, what had taken place had been like sword thrusts in the sky. Oh—there wasn't anything friendly about the way she watched me and waited for me. She was polite, because politeness authorized the greatest coldness. But I must say I wasn't getting up at that hour in order to obey the proprieties. I walked clumsily towards her, and she might have thought we were going to run straight into each other: I'm sure she was prepared to attack me, break my bones if she could and in any case stand up to me without yielding. She didn't budge at any moment. She didn't budge when I was close to her, either, close enough to see that she was still breathing, that she still had arteries and blood. But as soon as I said to her—and I said it calmly—"I've come to see your friend," she shuddered, as though she had been able to tolerate everything except for the truth to have a voice, and she ceased to be massive, unassailable. "My friend!" No irony in her voice, it seemed to me. Gravity, unshakable faith, made her extremely firm, but her intonation—a mixture of arrogance, questioning, triumph—was certainly intended to deny me the right to describe her relationships and at the same time victoriously seized my words to preserve them as a recognition of her rights. I think she allowed herself to be tempted by this word, because she repeated it, and this time really in order to listen to it herself, with a sort of uncertainty and happy surprise. In a sense, I had more allies in her than she wanted to admit and earthly fever was one of those allies. But she quickly freed herself and hurled at me under her breath: "Judith!" I listened to that, and I listened to it

13

without reacting, because, as often happened with her, seeing her defend not something small but her very life, I couldn't blame her. I only noticed the cunning way she let this name slip out, to make me understand that she was not fooled, and that the advantage I had given her by clumsily calling her her friend — well, I had done this in order to keep that name for myself. Yet her whisper made my uneasy; she had been afraid, she had groped her way towards something which, dauntless though she was, she was afraid to grasp: yes, she had placed her bet, slowly, without taking her eyes off me, as though in order to be able to withdraw it if the risk became too great. Then what was it? I admit that she found me out cruelly in my mistake.

All the more misguided since, an instant later, her attitude changed completely: she was still polite, but this politeness was seductive, unshadowed, capable of aimiably tolerating any amount of horror and impropriety. At this instant, she was perfect; the naturalness of her behavior protected her, and if she had done senseless things — and she must have — it all took place behind appearances that were too correct to invite comment. "I'll call her," she said, her eyes shining softly; she was protecting my behavior, but without intending anything unpleasant, simply in order to classify it with everyday truth that could be immediately realized. Well, I said to myself, she is almost beautiful; up till then I hadn't noticed it. What certainly has to be called her desire to conciliate was putting her face to face with a very conciliatory man; graciousness, comfort, were tranquilly enticing me into their game. Nevertheless, I asked her with some impertinence, since I wasn't forgetting the extraordinary, unlikely promptness with which she had taken up her position when I had just barely stood up: "But was I the one who woke you up?" "It's true — it's very late," she said brusquely, after rubbing her wrist under her eyes. "What is it?" she went on. "Are you in pain? You're not sleeping!" She passed quickly in

14

front of me and pushed against a door, saying: "I have an arsenal of sleeping pills in the kitchen." The kitchen? A cry rose up in me; the words "give me a glass of water" immediately came back to me and with them a feeling of terrible coldness. I went in after her, walking heavily as though I were continuing the journey of that afternoon. "Give me a glass of water," I said, quite ungraciously. At that moment she opened a small medicine cabinet, went over to another piece of furniture, took out a glass, wiped it. The kitchen wasn't large, and two people of our size would inevitably brush against each other. "Should I pour out some drops for you?" She was holding the half filled glass up as high as her face. At that instant she had the tone of voice of someone obeying powerful orders but without any authority herself. "No," I said to her, "not today!"

As I drank, I became aware of my thirst. The water was not only hours late in coming, it didn't get along very well with my thirst. I sat down on a stool and glanced at this woman. "It's a little late for water; I need some alcohol." But she gestured to me that there wasn't any. "There used to be!" No doubt this allusion to a time when a young man was in charge here seemed to her to come from a very comptemptible place, but one couldn't expect my thirst to be very considerate. The same state of mind started me on a cross-examination that was anything but subtle. However, to my surprise it led off with a declaration of good will:

"So tell me, my dear, is it such a bother for you to have me here now?"

Perhaps I wasn't in a position to watch her carefully, and it seems to me that during this whole time I saw her through my words, in some sense, but I think she blushed — slightly — probably because of that "my dear" which broke the windows between us so strangely. In any case, though she might have been able to allow herself to blush, her answer was steady:

15

"Why would it be?" she said boldly (though after a sober silence). "This sort of thing was to be expected. And at the moment it isn't much of a bother."

"At the moment! But do you think things are going to stay this way?"

She was quick to retort:

"They can! All they want is to stay this way—unless someone prevents them."

"Things, yes," I agreed, "they prefer that. And of course you would want that too?"

"Want what?" she asked, hesitating.

"Want things to stay this way!"

Emphatic though my question was, she didn't answer it; she seemed to resist expressing to me what she wanted or didn't want. So I clumsily went ahead:

"Really, would you like it, would you like it so much?"

"Yes," she said brusquely, "more than anything else in the world!"

The silence that followed this statement hardly showed how unexpected, how overwhelming it was, coming from her, how shaken I felt, how uneasy at having provoked it, and how from then on I kept at a respectful distance. How could I not comply with such frankness, such a loyal recognition of the truth? I said almost without thinking:

"Well, how are we going to get out of it now?"

"Get out of it?"

She seemed to have plunged—or was it I?—deep into the speech she had uttered; I could see clearly that now she was looking at me with those intense words, that she was affirmed, raised up in them, and now that she in turn was more than anything in the world, what she saw before her appeared to her only to be the shadow, which was doubtless immense, of her own immensity.

"Claudia," I said, and I stood up resolutely, "I'm afraid of being an inconvenience to you, of being more inconvenient than you're willing to admit. But now, neither one of us can ignore it any longer: something has happened."

"Something?"

"Yes. I'm here right now!"

"Certainly," she said with a confident smile. "You're here! Well, more or less."

"That's exactly right, more or less! That leaves you some margin. More or less! You have a right to choose, you know."

"The choice was made long ago," she said, staring at me with penetrating force.

"Really? You mean..."

"But you won't get out of it that way: you're here, you're here!" she added with fierce gaity. "Frankly, do you think it'll do you any good if..." She hesitated, I saw her wince painfully. It seems to me that I cried out to her: "Don't go any farther!" But she finished in a firm voice: "If you're only here for me."

I couldn't help it, I went close to her, close to this defiant speech, with which she was hurting herself just as much as me. Then what was behind this face? Only the desire for things to stay the way they were? The certainty that I was left out, that I was left out too? Strange face, that allowed itself to be looked at from very close, without yielding anything of its own accord; no, it wasn't even a reserved face, since all of it lay before my eyes, this cold image of my failure. At that instant I was struck by an astonishing recollection of things, all the more difficult because something there was escaping me, evading me, as though hastening not to warn me but to ignore me. I stood next to her, my back against the sink—just in front of me, the whitish pane of the medicine cabinet. Without looking at her and with some distress, I finally said:

"We're alone—is that what you want to make me say?"

"Well, more or less!" she said with the same liveliness. "Not really, of course. I suppose you wouldn't resign yourself to the inevitable, and I..." Her voice weakened to a painful tremor, then rose again on the other side of what she seemed to have expressed without bothering to say it. "Otherwise," she continued, "we wouldn't be here together, and this conversation would be out of place."

"It seems to me that you don't have much sympathy for the character you're conversing with?"

"It's true. I could say to you: not yet. But I'm afraid things will stay this way." She remained silent for a moment. "I think it would be better not to leave this hanging: I am ignoring dissipated feelings, and I'm not interested in what goes on in your world."

Still, I was surprised by the stiffness of her explanation.

I simply said to her, "I'm sorry I can't say exactly the same thing to you, but you won't suffer from it, even if I stay. And now, be frank about this too: wouldn't you really like to see me go? Wouldn't you be relieved if all of a sudden I was far away, as far away as possible?"

The question took her by surprise, for a moment she seemed to be dreaming.

"You mean: leave for good?"

"For good!"

"But would you do it?"

"Yes, I'm prepared to do it."

"Would you promise? No," she said, shaking her head, "I don't believe you, all men are deceitful, all men lie. You lie too, I know it."

"Really! How do you know it?"

"I know it, I know it," she said stubbornly. "I would never be convinced that you were gone for good and that you were far way."

"Don't believe me. I won't swear to it, just for you. I'll leave if that's better, and I'll come back if that's better. But whether or not you think my words are deceitful, let me say this: I'll go and you won't hear any more talk about me if that will really straighten things out for you."

"For me?"

"For both of you."

That upset her more seriously than I had thought it would. A sort of flame, a violent, proud and jealous fire rose in her eyes, which became very black:

"I want you to know," she said in her high voice, "that it won't make any difference to me whether you're here or not. My life won't be changed by it except in ways that don't matter to it, and what's important to it won't be changed. I'll see you, if I have to, and not without some enjoyment, because I'll find it pleasant to talk to you, since you didn't come to see me. What I have, I'll always have: you won't take it away from me. What you don't have, what you've lost, you'll never have again. You said it: we're alone, but you're more alone that I am!"

I think that was more or less what she said, but I won't really swear to it because she had hardly finished her tirade—which had something theatrical about it—as in her anger she was prepared to shower me with even more terrible truths—was it anger? or a need, a desperate energy—when an incident occurred that shouldn't have been in the least unexpected and that nevertheless startled me so, and her too, that I threw myself on her arm like a madman and held her as hard as I could, without her trying to free herself. This incident, which followed her spirited outburst, was that the bedroom door opened. We were struck by this, both of us were overwhelmed, as though this were the strangest thing; perhaps because the noise was so slight, so timid, so different from the din of our voices; or perhaps all of a sudden the strangeness of that silent creaking several feet away, out of our sight, engraved upon the reality of the space of the night the undivulged strangeness of what we had been looking for beneath our words and could discuss calmly as along as this was taking place inside us, but that struck us, struck me with surprise and her with a sort of terror, as soon as we were in danger of seeing something appear outside, in the real proximity of the night open behind us, that was also behind our thoughts. I am sure of this, and the fact that we were both startled was evidence: for her and for me, at that moment, what began to move, to open the door so silently, was nothing less terrible than *a thought,* and no doubt it was quite different for each of us, but in that instant we at least had this much in common, that neither of us was capable or worthy of enduring it. After a moment, I gestured to her, I indicated that I was going to go out quietly. She looked at me in a sort of unconscious way; but as soon as I moved she caught me back, she held me close to her with incredible nervous strength. Was it fear? A reawakening of life? Rather—and this came into my thoughts right away—even though the slight creaking was not followed by another noise, she must have seen that just on the other side there was a timid and frightened expectation that my abrupt approach could take by surprise in a dangerous way: she had the finest instinct for all that; she gave the impression of knowing, better than anyone and better than I, what could happen behind a wall, as if, by sheer force of attention, by having, day and night, spied upon and kept watch over what was escaping her, she had succeeded in reconquering a portion of reality. So I stayed there, tightly held by her, my eyes fixed on the kitchen door. I was beginning to feel ill at ease in the grip of this feverish hand, which kept me from continuing to move away. Now it was no longer possible to go over there, calmly and naturally, in broad daylight, as I should have. I fully realized that the silence here might seem very strange on the other side, now that the night had opened, and the longer we let it go on, the more it became difficult to break, the more it became wrong and, in a word, culpable. I had detected that right away, when she had made me take part in her fear, the complicity of her surprise and that impulse towards concealment we both had in the face of something that demanded the gesture of truth. Maybe she had not calculated anything and I was only being confronted with my own dissimulation and the lack of concern I had shown for true things during that conversation; but the result was the same, and she was the only one who benefitted: I had allowed myself to be caught out between those two silences, one of them separate, exiled, lost in a distance without resources, the other avid, jealous, implacable—and the latter, with which I had nothing in common but an instant's agreement, finally imposed itself on me to such an extent that it made me inseparable from it and resembled the profoundness of an inadmissable fault, I saw this clearly when she let go of me and walked forward by herself, without bothering about me and without any fear of being followed, and went quite naturally into the front hall and a little later into the bedroom, closing the door.

If it hadn't been so great, the deception would have been final. I would have left. I, too, would have gone into the front hall, and from there rejoined the tranquil flow of the rue de la Victoire and gone down towards the Opéra, which I liked at that hour, and I would have been happy. I could see very clearly what kind of light shone on the square, I could see the motion of those streets at such a moment, not furtive, as people think, but familiar and full of kindness; these are the most beautiful hours in the world, hours in which anyone would cheerfully tolerate living an endless life. I said to myself: in an instant I will be down there, and I felt a burst of immense pleasure. The day! These instants of the night-time street are the glory of the day, the wood fire that is already burning and in which each person dissipates and burns in

21

the shiver of a day that doesn't yet know itself. I saw that, I was experiencing that, having already experienced it. These hours were within my reach, hours that asked nothing of me and of which I asked nothing except that they go by without touching me and that they ignore me after having known me. And it's true, they went by happily without me; and I too, unknown to them, went joyfully by, ignored, ignoring the eternal: alone? alone! My decline could accommodate everything.

This continued, the old farce: the last moment, so happy it was on the verge of never being the last. I recognized it, still perfectly happy, with its brightness, its freest and most joyful brightness, but now it was joyfully distant behind the pane of glass, caught up again in the flow of the world, without bitterness at having been put at stake like me. What is a night, after all? It shouldn't seem surprising that I arose from these hours with a feeling of inexpressible pleasure. Yes, this motion had crossed the night, it had been born then, of the good faith of the hours, of the fullness of deception, and it was born again of the dark future, of the trickery of time, and above all of the fact that there would never again be such a great deception. Deception was not possible; I tranquilly discovered that in the morning.

As far as I remember—but I recall only that immense calm: it might well be that the new day opened on what I called Claudia's side, the obligation to respond, politely, to the polite help she gave me, the return to the bathroom, the certainty that my presence was terribly "out of place," as she had said, then the impression that from then on I would have to play a role, if only the comic role that, through her (I was her guest, in any case), would be designed by the appearances of a reasonable life, using me as a model. All this, and the sleep that came, and on the other side of the sleep the noises, the fatigue of the footsteps I went on hearing, probably in the bathroom, fugitive faces that approached and receded, the feeling of an indistinct attention of

22

which I was the center and the thing at stake, this was not the hovering of a hostile surveillance, but something worse that resembled, curiously, the memory of that nervous grip by which I had been held back and even now, in all the dangerous slipping of sleep, still continued to be held back, always saved at the last moment by the decision of an implacable energy: even though these impressions, and a thousand others, all close to fever, to truthless chattering, to the sarcastic erosion of time, dropped on me again and again, terrifying to the fruitless work of the sleeper, all of them also dropped into the same calm which, not being repose at all, but something deep and alive, reconciled them in the wildness of its eddies. Even Claudia did not escape this calm, or perhaps it only existed between her and me, showing her to be less tense, less polite too, perhaps more agitated, coming in and going out somewhat at random, like someone who accepts the law of time and no longer prepares to leap beyond necessity. Maybe she was more sure of herself now, more sure of me, for she had been able to gauge my weaknesses, but that wasn't like her, she didn't slacken so easily, she certainly didn't believe she was the winner just because she had prevailed over one night, she heard, better than anyone, with her sharp ears, all the quiet noises attacking the thickness of the night that she had raised between me and her destiny. And there weren't really so many problems. I can swear that by letting it pass with all its wonted tranquillity, by giving it the right to linger indefinitely in the moments it preferred, without provoking it with questions like these—"What's going to happen now? and tomorrow? after that? but shouldn't I . . ."—this life glided by in the most natural way, and if it had some difficult moments, they were caused by one or the other of us beginning to force it, and trying, since after all one had to get it over with, to make it result in something.

Naturally, this wasn't defensible, and we certainly weren't

there in order to help make our little community stay on its feet: on the contrary, each of us was relying on the imminence of the ending—imminence that had nothing to do with duration—but leaned on it with such force that the edifice of an instant, founded on nothing, could also appear extremely solid. No one had produced this state of things, I mean no one turned around to contemplate it. I don't know what people on the outside thought of it: surely nothing, since they saw nothing, but I have to add that those on the inside were also not disposed to look over their shoulders, to give up the depth of their lives, especially at such a moment, for the pleasure of a rigorous judgment. It was all too certain that this judgment prowled around me, a temptation, a trap in which I couldn't let myself be caught at any price, and even now that I have tied it down, I can control only what I say, not what I have seen. From then on, and even though sometimes I was so close to seeing everything that I had to commit myself to a terrible attempt at passivity just so as not to lose myself in this vision of everyone, from that moment on—and this was undoubtedly the result of a long history, but even more the result of something that wasn't my doing and that I think I won't fathom completely until the time comes, until the proper moment comes—I too had won the right to stick firmly to the passion of my look, to that alone, even if my look was sterile and not very happy.

Were we waiting? I don't think so, or if we were, it was in our singularly prudent behavior in regard to time, which mostly consisted of each of us in our own way—and the ways were very different—appeasing it by making each moment a kind of uneasiness that was afterwards ignored. One way things had a chance of lasting was that the only really active person exert herself to let things stay the way they were. For reasons that weren't very clear—this was one of the areas I didn't want to turn towards—as though she had had the idea that we had reached a point where it was no longer possible to go back, at least not directly, and she had to stop everything with a powerful determination, petrify the situation, or else prolong it, isolate it in such a way that nothing could happen to it except under her control and in keeping with her views, or else in the hope that once it was cut off from its source and floating adrift, this situation, so threatening, would end up disintegrating into a mediocrity that had no future: were these her reasons? Mine, really; something was driving her, something I couldn't fathom. But if it wasn't clear to me what she had in mind, I did see clearly how skilfully she had coached appearances—right away, during the very time I was sleeping—and established around us the setting of a solid existence.

Far too shrewd, moreover, to seem to be the one taking action (whether grudgingly or quite voluntarily), just as she never showed that she intended to encompass the future. As for my visit, it seems to me there was no question of making it interminable by foreseeing that it would last. At the very most, things arranged themselves in such a way that the idea of leaving and even the memory of my arrival had no place there, for the moment—but only for the moment, and because this limited the perspective to a very brief time, it gave the moment an extraordinary poise. As far as I can see there were moments, some very agreeable, others more painful, on which I felt myself to be so firmly established, far from any horizon, that if I had been questioned about the reasons for my presence, I would have answered bravely: "Well, things are still continuing!" They did more than just continue, but even in the more precise observations I could formulate to myself about what "exactly" was happening, in these observations of the moment, which were sufficient for me, for the side of myself that looked at the world, I recognized an authority that went far beyond appearances and resulted from their distant glimmer in the past.

I think we were playing games with one another, but with as little trickery as possible. If I wanted to describe to myself the ways in which each of us was behaving, at first I would see only this strange fact: there was understanding among us. Moments that are still present to me and always astonishingly simple and happy. Certainly neither Claudia nor I, who both had afterthoughts, would have been capable of capturing such a correct tone: in spite of everything, she was inclined to keep an eye on me, and I was inclined to evade her. But in the tapistry work we were composing thread by thread with our gestures—a tapestry well suited to the decor of a museum—our stiffness and our strained behavior disappeared because of the perfectly natural life that flowed between us. I must say, though, that in such an apparently false situation, this naturalness really resembled a spell cast by the memory of the truth on beings who were much less true. Where I was concerned, I could not be very perceptive either, nor very difficult. I had decided to say no more about it. And having decided that, what was left of me seemed to be occupied only with looking at a face, touching a body—and not at all with holding onto it, even less with asking questions to find out what that face saw of me. On my part, it was the movement of haste, the liveliness of an instant that no longer bothers about anything. What was I asking? At certain moments, I could have found such a face quite reserved, such a contact quite distant, and such perfect kindness strangely divided. But these moments had no place in my existence, which was always reduced to a single moment: a unique moment, marvelously agreeable and important, that made me feel that all of space, from the remotest point to the nearest, was entirely occupied by the living reality of one face, and opened the world for me to the immense measure of that face. Anyone who lives elsewhere has nothing, but elsewhere was not questioning me. One touch, the most momentary, and through it I fiercely drew to myself the certainty and the intimacy of a limitless consent—I needed nothing more than that, and I was nothing more, and surely nothing else continued to exist, beyond one confine after another, that was as worthy of the name of universe: I could not be lured into that, at least as long as the energy of that instant lasted.

It may be that I'm deluding myself about the quality of our understanding, and perhaps under what I call understanding is really the exaltation and ignorance of my own gesture. I can't decide, but that doesn't change in any way the fact that those moments were moments of ignorance and not a fight to the death. I recall very clearly that there was something animated and lively between us. For example, I see this image: above the piano and opposite me was hanging a portrait of Judith dating from a period when I didn't yet know her; it was a splendid work that I was looking at with pleasure (this must have happened at the end of the morning). The wood was beginning to catch fire somewhere to my right, somewhere, but closer—I could touch it—a live body, standing, that must have been turned towards the fire; the wood burned boldly with a flame that thickened the daylight. I stretched out my hand toward this body, fell to the level of her hips, and was burned by the dry, vegetable heat (radiating from the fire), which gave me the impression that she was roasting nicely without noticing it. I said this to her. But I was extremely happy that for my sake she had saturated herself with all the logs' fire so as to offer me this single vivifying point, the blazing end of a twig. She loved the fire, she was very capable where anything to do with the life of the fire was concerned, it was one of the tasks reserved for her, and she was going to make something superb of this one, an immense flame, she said as she stood up again, because she had kneeled to look at it more closely. "Look, look!" Unsettled, she showed me the complicity of the piece of wood going up in flames, and for me too, it was unsettling, that shiver of storm.

At which moments, then, had the amiable conventions been overstepped? I can't say exactly, but on this very morning I think they had already disappeared. One of the signs— afterwards this changed—was that we were together most of the time, like people who were indispensable to one another. One can't help admiring this sensible solution. Since necessity had tugged at us dangerously to put us under the same roof, it would have been ridiculous to pretend to escape it by scattering into different corners of an apartment as big as a pocket handker-chief. Discretion, reserve—this was what threatened to throw us at one another, not a frank recognition of the reality. When I discovered that the fact of not being with Claudia expressed itself—not always, it's true—in the various ailments I've mentioned—and I wasn't surprised, I found it natural that, hav-ing so completely taken charge of her life in a difficult period, Claudia was still called upon sometimes to help—well, I took the simplest course. I didn't want to start up again with "What's the matter, what's the matter," nor torment with questions a trou-ble that didn't want to show itself. I also think that at such a moment I wasn't tempted to carry on conversations: too much time was needed for that, too much indifference, a taste for the future, and my desire went through the instant and through ignorance, not through knowledge.

Yes, those moments were singularly charming. The two of them were living there before my eyes, and the naturalness of the one inspired the other with a rare and wonderful kindness. In my memory that liveliness is wedded to the morning light. The sun shone into the studio until two o'clock. We often ate lunch late, and when it was over I was already tense and in a more somber mood. In the afternoon, I heard the sound of Claudia's voice, a voice that was beautiful but without happiness, that was not easy to listen to without having certain reservations. She sang in several languages (she herself was a foreigner), I don't think she sang simply or even always tastefully; if she became excited, which happened when I found the strength to accompany her, she was excessively theatrical. Perhaps in the midst of her successes she had always been this sublime and tiresome singer who didn't know her real talent. Peculiar gifts, revealed by a sudden coldness, a more abstract rendering, like an imperceptible distancing of the voice. The pathos of the deeper registers had nothing to do with this event. I had heard voices harmoniously bound to desolation, to anonymous misery, I had been attentive to them, but this one was indifferent and neutral, hidden away in a vocal region where it stripped itself so completely of all superfluous perfections that it seemed deprived of itself: her voice was true, but in such a way that it reminded one of the sort of justice that has been handed over to all negative hazards. Short instants, perhaps; certainly, nothing touching or interesting; a little thing that didn't bother about the quality of works, that happened behind the music—and yet an instant of the music—and that communicated...well, what? Really, it communicated very little. Her friend said to her: "You're in poor voice" or "Your voice is thin," and other phrases that dated from her days in the theater. I myself didn't notice what the value of that poor voice was. The ceremony of singing tired me (for a long time singing had been a disappointing area for me); I put up with the gaity, the nothingness of the words, but that glorious voice, the royal interment, returned me in a commanding way to a museum existence. Naturally it was possible not to listen to it; I wondered if she was worried about that, being heard; perhaps she missed the theater, off hand her retirement seemed unreasonable, but was she retired? She had mentioned recording sessions, maybe she was rehearsing at that very moment; yes, she must have been working; that explained why she wasn't really singing, but rather looking for something that would be the beginning, the hope of her own singing. At the time

29

I had the impression that she was holding back, the better to decipher a difficult text. This discovery, the feeling of being useless to her singing, since she was studying, the slow progress of the day, which was already almost dark: yielding to these emotions, I think I was struck by something that became a cloud, but a remarkable cloud, remarkably solid and real. As I watched it come forward, I had the impression that I had heard it often before—she was singing a smooth and distant sort of German—and this impression passed before me, for all of us a stronger light that twisted around and illuminated us from underneath. *Es fällt kein Strahl.* At that instant I must have discovered that it wasn't possible for her to need to work on a piece like that, such a classic. Her voice was marvelous, of an extraordinary restraint: it, too, had folded its wings, and its flight, deep inside a rarer element, continued to seek the simple happiness of singing, while she herself impassively expected— and affirmed—that the singing would not begin.

I don't recall having expressed any opinion about this to her, at least not then; she didn't expect it and I didn't expect it of myself either. Usually, and this was one of the happy aspects of that life, she didn't ask anything of me, she avoided challenging me. In the way she spoke in front of me without speaking for me there was a suggestion that I took to be the desire not to impose their life on me any more than I wanted. It seems to me that lasted quite a long time. Part of the morning, when the "dish of tea" had gone back to the kitchen, was spent in joyful careless-ness between the bedroom and the bathroom, but she was not at all embarrassed to go into the studio too, with apparently just as much freedom as though this man, who was a stranger to her, didn't have eyes with which to see her, and this freedom was not even characteristic of her friend. What was surprising was not these free ways but the discretion with which all this happened, approached, receded, became an image veiled, unveiled, and yet still veiled by a certain impersonal air; imperceptibly, she had placed a feeling of reserve between us that left her and left me much freer than any wall, because behind a screen my gaze could always have looked for her, but now, when it found her mulling over her clothes, it found nothing but the phrase "It's her," which naturally couldn't be practically naked.

Each of them had her own household duties. "I'll do this." "I'll do that." These duties were just as important as the large projects of the future, they were solemn decisions that referred to another world. "I'll go buy some wood!" "I'll go to the laundry!" "I'll speak to the concierge!" All this flew over their two cups, in the morning, like eternal vows. "The vacuum cleaner!" "The leak!" "The blocked up garbage chute!" And the conclusion, the dismal end of every venture: "Madame Moffat will get rid of all that." The doors slammed, banged. The chilly air, ferreting about, ran behind them wherever they went, busy, idle, with no other role but to wrap their comings and goings in a fringe of cloth. They walked around a lot, both of them had a certain instability. It was like a treasure hunt, with backtrackings, halts, dives into water, whispers through space, a roving pursuit that could have no other object than to obscure the trail and irritate the pursuers. "When will it be found?" It was already found! Here, and here, constantly. Sometimes she came in staring at her hands: "Now what was I looking for!" A handkerchief, a brush, a pin? It didn't matter, every time it was a treasure, enough for those empty hands. "Gently, now," a voice murmured. "Gently?" The awakening, an immense calm.

This occurred to me: that when I woke up, I found someone close to me. This was certainly part of the charm of the first moments. But I couldn't explain to myself why this idea was so worrying.

I must say that something else, something more serious, was worrying me. Can I say what it was? I would have to be able to go

31

back to a true beginning. I asked—in vain—for help at a particular moment, on a particular day. "At a given moment," as they say; but when was the moment given to me?

Yet my confusion became so great that I tried, not to clear it up, but to make it pass into my life. I had no lack of strength, I busied myself with my little jobs, everyone lives that way. I would sometimes stare through the window for a long time at the disfigured facade of the synagogue (one shouldn't forget the bomb)—that black wall, those beams supporting the entrance or closing it off, a merciless image. Certainly the truth does not die easily.

Because we lived together, I also looked at Judith's face. Familiarity did not wear it out in the least. Beautiful? I think it was, but looking at it isn't the same as describing it. (I certainly didn't photograph it. And I'm convinced that I didn't look at it in order to attribute feelings to it.) Nevertheless, I will say something about it: I found her extraordinarily visible. She appeared—and this was a fascinating, inexhaustible pleasure.

What made the situation terrifying was that I—and surely each of us—was at the very limit of happy feelings. We could have gone even farther? But why? For the sake of what? Farther! Farther was exactly where we were. Desire wanted it? Desire also wanted eternity.

I had woken up feeling a terrible shiver, all awakenings are more or less associated with a shiver. But this one was a greater force, fierce and facetious, and I fully realized it. I was infinitely indebted to it. Without it, what would my desire have been? A lonesome mimicry, grimacing. But it had uplifted me, and because it was the day, its trembling was the trembling of the day. To illuminate, to make something appear, yes; to see, an immense pleasure; but to continue desiring right up to the end—only a shiver like that could make me believe this was possible.

I got up and walked a few steps toward the window. Since the fire had been laid, I had had no trouble lighting the wood, but in the bathroom I became disoriented by the cold and a cave-like darkness (there was no electricity that day); the trembling—the shiver was no more than this trembling—stretched out in me with a rather strange slowness, like a heavy layer, not very icy, like a voice softer than mine, which made the invasion hardly disagreeable. And yet I staggered. I had to go back to the other room, I didn't have the impression I was walking, I was drinking space, I was turning it into water; drunk? gorged with emptiness. I peacefully sank down onto the carpet; I half slept; shortly afterwards, I got dressed without mishap, except that if I moved at all briskly I was caught up again by the astounding transport of that shiver, which hadn't left me at all.

The continuation? Unfortunately this isn't a story. When I discovered that I was bound to this avid day, perhaps I had hoped, in my impatience, my excess of patience, that from now on it would manage things. "Let the shiver decide," that's what our fondness for rest leads us to say. But I had an excuse: the capriciousness, the strangeness of its force. It certainly gave me no orders, it didn't forbid me anything—either to involve myself with space, or to do as I liked—but when the time came, at the right moment, it scattered me through one abyss after another, although—and this was what was strange—this did not seem to me to go beyond the truth of a shiver. My strength was betraying me, but what was it being unfaithful to? To its own limits: it was excessive, hopelessly great.

I threw a piece of wood on the fire. I felt very bad now. I was losing strength quickly. Once I had returned to my bed—but I remained beside it, standing, I had in some sense lost the ability to lie down. Now and then I was shaken by convulsive yawns, spasms far too large for a mouth. Did I want air? I would have been better off falling. But instead of that, I was stirred by an astonishing rage, and failing myself, whom I would have wanted to hurl against the door, I seized around the waist a miserable thing, vaguely white, that had been present throughout this whole scene and that was dissipated by the force of the impact. It was blown out like a light. The impression I had—an effect of my stupor—was that there was an empty spot there, but also, which was very depressing, that something was caught in a trap—between heaven and earth, as they say, I thought these words in German, *zwischen Himmel und Erde*. I must have calmly lain down shortly afterwards.

No doubt "calmly" meant that at this point everything could begin again. It is true that I revived an irritation (to call it that) which, lying down as I was, turned me into a violently constricted private place. As I shook my shoulders and surmised that the strange shiver lurking around there seemed already to have become docile and inoffensive, I was moved by fury: already it was yielding—and to me, to the authority that was being exercised in me despite me. A man who needs the wind in order to burn is always allowed to open the window, to throw himself out. But "calmly" made fun of such childishness.

Another irritating impression: it was broad daylight, and that should be understood to mean precisely a day of broad light. I was watching it, since I had nothing else to do; behind the pane, something surprising seemed to be taking place; what? I wasn't in a very good position to realize this, but the anomaly was visible. Fog, I thought—then I saw that it was beginning to snow, an event that gave me no pleasure at all and that even irritated me like a badly timed joke.

I couldn't deceive myself, there was something rather disturbing about this irritation (and hard to endure): a cry, but too violent, an infinite and voiceless vibration. Is this what thought is—this strength choked by weakness? Then I was thinking dangerously. I was extremely cold. The fire had probably gone out. I recalled that fire with a feeling of sympathy—it had allowed itself to be lit so easily a short time before, and during a snowfall. The flakes had been followed by powder, and the powder by an attractive, radiant outdoors, something too manifest, an insistent appearance, almost an apparition—why that? Was the day trying to show itself?

A little later (I think) my feeling of irritation became quite unreasonable; it may be that this feeling and the snow were connected. The monotony of the outdoors was not a violent chaos, as happens during blizzards, and which would have lent its strength to mine, but in the face of such an excessive inconsistency, more and more fruitless and oppressive, my exasperation mounted in a fantastic way, and yet I was calm, I didn't budge: nothing could have been more terrible. Here the phenomenon of the windowpane was playing a strange game. The snow wasn't stopping there, it was really coming into the room, but was it snow? only its perverse side, something insignificant, shameless and deceitful, though alive. The free air! I thought. Of course, I couldn't appeal to the others. The others were coming and going, in their endless happiness. Doors were banging, shutters were opening: "Look at the snow!" The fire sparkled and burned. The cold? The happiness, the warmth of the cold. My pulse was beating joyfully too. And the marvellous whisper: "Snow, like my country..." "Winter, yet again..." Go farther? Here and here, at each instant.

I could have stood up and broken the windowpanes, flown into a rage, as they say—I think I had enough strength for that. Surely, inside this terrible patience that kept me quiet in the midst of a furious desire, there was a temptation to speak, a terrible, dramatic temptation to denounce this calm, to pronounce one word, the final truth of a word; but I did not speak; it seems to me, in spite of what the books say, that I never spoke. Out of weakness? Out of respect for feelings of happiness? I didn't want to slander with the truth what was even truer—and also, I'm not a judge. It wasn't up to me to speak.

I never spoke, but "never" could end at any instant; "never," a very close limit for someone burning with impatience. At a certain moment, as Claudia passed near me "by chance," the same chance induced her to stop and look at me—in a very instructive way, I mean that she was finding out about me, because of me, my nearness, and I was also being taught in my own way, in some sense I was learning something new (this didn't have to relate to her: new, but also in a free state, a luminous, intermittent particle). Question her? Because of the cold—and there was no electric current for the radiator—our tasks were suspended, or turned into amusements: by this one could tell that the day was perverse. I think that certain ways in which they behaved had never been serious, this lack explained why life was so cheerful. Even if an incident occurred (as Claudia was running a comb through her friend's hair, I had seen her friend dodge away from her with a *sudden motion, with an almost wild leap*), this scene—the hair pulled unintentionally, the angry reaction—belonged to the world of the cheerful life: a lovable caprice, without any importance (but when the law of seriousness has ceased to be imposed, everything becomes extremely important); there was nothing about the scene that could turn it into a real difficulty. I watched them running the brush and comb through each other's hair, turn and turn about, a ceremony with a thousand variations, which stretched out indefinitely. What I saw in this image was an antidote to the dissolving eternity of the snow, a remedy, a game in which time was being put at stake. Surely I had to take this sight into consideration. Was I under an enchantment? Yes, a joyous obligation, the obligation to stay here in order to perpetuate what I was seeing: the thousand variations of the ceremony, Claudia joyously tousling her hair, reminding it of how it used to be arranged, though this hair didn't remember its history at all, so that the game didn't go any farther than approximations, fluffy parodies, under which the expression on her face was accentuated, the atavistic look that didn't seem to be really hers but rather mirrored an aspect of the earth, the inexhaustible resource drawn out by these attempts at disguise. A face like that was hardly made to be seen, I was seeing it unlawfully, in a sense, "by chance," even though at such a moment the whole scene seemed to be taking place only for the sake of this apparition. At such a moment? And when did that moment begin? Nevertheless, it was at just such a moment, with a suddenness I was aware of, a suddenness so dazzling that it took all the power away from the phrase "all at once": I found myself seized again, caught up again by the sudden motion, the *almost wild leap* I spoke of and that took the form of a bolt of lightning. Without my being able to understand exactly when it happened, this sudden movement shook me, I was overcome with horror; I think I saw light, a vision difficult to sustain, instantaneous, connected to that movement, as though the fact that the two of them were torn apart, as though this cruel space . . . but I can't do it, I can't finish the sentence. I had stood up; I almost fell to the floor. Thank God, I was on the point of dying, these words were not a discovery but, as they crossed my fall, they were revealed under a piercing light, as a sort of oracle choking my strength and goading it into this pitilessly ample vibration: "Death! But in order to die, one had to write—The end! And to do that, one had to write up to the end."

I don't know if this shock set off in me what people call a period of remission. To a certain extent, it was the start of a new era, a tragic one in many respects, but since this shock wandered about freely, it seems hard to take it as a reference point for any sort of beginning. I have never hidden it—it was terrible, terrible, because of its powerful impact which, before it touched me, swept time away, and yet I fell into this open well down to the dizzying heart of time, to a pitilessly precise date, and the same date, though it is hard to know if I was coming to it through an effort against my energy or if it was taking hold of me again because in reality time had not passed. This was one of the thoroughly painful aspects of this event, even though there were others I can't speak of directly. Furthermore, what made it a wild motion was that no matter how much it repeated itself, it wasn't really repeating itself; it wasn't really its own life; and besides, up to a certain point it took into account the orientation of the days and of everyday circumstances, even though the latter were quite fascinated by this unexpected power, even as they tried their best to go on playing their part. I make this observation now, because now, when I found myself back at the same point, soaked in sweat—I had dreamed that I was lying in bathwater—I had an attack of profound weakness. In fact, I had felt this moment coming for a long time. I had managed to say no more about it, to stifle the useless questions about what "exactly" happened, because of my inflamed energy. But now, in this bathtub-shaped ditch which I had been lowered into at a certain moment and where I had been abandoned as though inadvertantly, I saw the light from so far away, and it was such a narrow light, so irresolute and detached, that I let go of myself, because after all it is inevitable, and what immediately corresponded to this letting go—naturally I barely realized this—was a cold, indifferent lucidity. Yet I remember what extraordinary sadness this moment brought me. I had lost all my impatience. I felt rather well. This was how I answered a question someone asked me: "Oh no, I'm perfectly fine."

Soaked in sweat, I wanted to go back into the bathroom and immerse myself in the water. I had a vague idea that during an earlier attempt I had been deflected and that I had to set out all over again from there. But when I stood up, I discovered that it

38

was still snowing; I think I let out an amazing cry, almost a howl; I threw myself on Claudia, who also, it seems to me, spoke more than a few words. Even though there was nothing to indicate that the amplitude of my leap had to stop there—it was clearly capable of carrying me much farther—she restrained me firmly and I found myself once again tightly held against her. I was left with a striking memory, if a dim one, of this motion, even though it was unfairly cut short. I should add that her presence, which was, for me, intimately included from the very beginning in the vision of "it went on snowing," gave me pleasure. I quickly recovered. I wanted to drink and eat, especially drink. Judith was sent to the kitchen to make some tea, a drink I had little taste for, but I put up with it.

While I drank the tea—it was insipid, sweet, bitter, a sad mixture—I returned to a sort of silence (earlier, I think I had thrown myself into a conversation that was barely under control and over which still floated a grandiose satisfaction). What was in this silence? A question, probably. I couldn't get through the cup of tea. Since I was dressed, I gave up on the water and contented myself with taking a few steps toward the window: it was still snowing, a dense, serious snow, but now I hardly bothered very much about this amazing event. Yet I remained there as long as I could, my forehead at the same height as the deep masses of snow, but I couldn't get through it any more than I could the tea.

Question her? But about what? It wasn't possible that the element of uneasiness and tragic difficulty in my presence passed unnoticed. And yet, who was alluding to it? Who was helping me become aware of it? Perhaps I didn't look like a man who doesn't know what to do? I was certainly calm, and no more calm than necessary, at the level of the calm that was the natural element of the world. At length, I had this impression: I had returned to my bed (but I wasn't lying down); Judith, who was

39

standing, continued to look out the window. I experienced a slight feeling of cold, not the overwhelming cold of a shiver, but a calm, silent cold (once again everything was plunged in a special silence). Perhaps this was because Claudia (she came in carrying some wood) stopped and looked at me in her instructive way, but I can't say it any other way: during the whole time she watched me, I understood that I was out there, in the slight, calm, and in no way disagreeable cold of the outdoors, and that I was looking at her from out there, through the transparency of the frost, in the same profound and silent way.

I will be more explicit about this right now: it was only an idea, the truth of a sensation. It would certainly have been simpler for me at that instant to be a face that belonged to the outdoors plunging into the room and looking questioningly at the people who were there, and no doubt I actually had that sensation, I really had it, but the thing is that perhaps this face was all I could grasp then and all the others could tolerate of the truth: this was why it had its chance. I ask myself this today (groping, for there is a time for seeing and a time for knowing). I ask myself why that distant and tranquil face—which I didn't see, but through whose approach a certain view approached me—presented itself, persisted as a permissible allusion to an event that didn't tolerate any allusion. In the darkness of time, it seems to me that this had been decided in me: I knew everything, and now I had perhaps forgotten everything except the terrible certainty that I knew everything. I couldn't ask questions, I don't think I had the slightest idea what a question might be, and yet it was necessary to ask questions, it was an infinitely great need. How could I have avoided this "tragic difficulty"? How could I not have done everything possible to express it and give it life? And then what was I if not this reflection of a face that didn't speak and that no one spoke to, capable of nothing more, as it rested on the endless tranquillity of the outdoors, than silently questioning the world from the other side of a window-pane?

This is why I must say something else. I had returned to my bed. Judith, who was standing, looked attentively out the window, and while she was there, staring as I had done at the deep masses of snow, I myself made a discovery too, calm, passionless (everything, as I said, was plunged in a special silence): that she was looking out the window (not at me), and the proof of the intensity, the intimacy of her gaze, was the silence that nothing could disturb any more than she herself could be disturbed from her watching. And what about me, can I say that I saw her? No, not completely, only from the back, her head three quarters turned away, her hair glossy and unkempt on her shoulders. It seems to me it was at that instant that Claudia, who had come in, looked at me in order to "break the spell," and it was also then that, in the slight cold of the outdoors, I in turn stared at her through the transparency of the frost and questioned her silently.

In what spirit did Claudia go along with this change? She must have had her reasons. When she saw her friend looking out the window so attentively (looking out the window being a phrase she used), she probably didn't feel very happy. I imagine that she didn't like this window, but that she respected it as Judith's own truth, and no doubt for her the day was empty, but she certainly didn't care, it was quite enough for her to look at the one who was looking, this was the one she was interested in and not a strange image, kept dreadfully close by the strength of desire but inaccessible all the same. This last circumstance must have played a part in her compliance. I wonder if she was not trying to enclose the truth, represent it in this remarkably ironic situation: I was there in flesh and blood, but Judith continued to look out the window at me in a sterile way.

I must have noticed—but at what moment?—that it was a

constant subject of conversation between the two of them. I had always sensed the existence of a secret, of a sort of preestablished language, and the fact that often I didn't have the key to what they were saying hardly mattered to me, because I didn't trouble myself over spoken things. But it is likely that soon after the instant in which I made that dive upwards—that leap, that surprised and joyous leap towards the words "it was still snowing," which Claudia despotically succeeded in restraining—I must also have realized this: that far from coming out of the fog, I had well and truly plunged into a region of the darkest preoccupations, the darkest images and words.

And what about me, was I in on the secret? At the very most, I was the secret, and for that reason quite far removed from having anything to do with it. And this was probably what I had begun to discover: that I was excluded from it.

I stayed in my corner without moving. The snow had turned into a deep gloom again. On her knees, Claudia was waiting for the logs to make up their minds.

"Well," she said, "it hasn't worked yet."

I asked:

"Could I go to the bathroom? Has the electricity come on again?"

"Why," she said, laughing, "go without light!"

"You know, your bathroom is like a cellar."

The weather was turning wet, and the shopping was put off until later.

I said to Claudia, "Don't you have amazing boots that come up to your knees?"

"Completely ordinary boots, the kind all the women there have. The truth is that the North attracts you, you're a man of the North."

"Yes, but I'm afraid of the cold."

It's true, I suffered from the cold. Did I shiver? It was a cold that didn't play around with shivers. I stood up, walked between the two of them.

"Does either one of you have a pencil?"

Claudia stood up, whistling to herself.

"It has several colors," she said, fiddling with her mechanical pencil. "It doesn't work very well." When I put out my hand, she grabbed me by the wrist with a little capricious gesture: "Don't bother with that. You're much better, you know; you're not going to die. Take a good look at her."

She meant her friend.

"You had an argument this morning," I said.

"Oh! You noticed, you're very observant. And naturally you were pleased?"

"No, I don't like it. I'd rather you got along."

"Now, now, you two!" she said with a little sneer.

"Why are you calling me 'tu'?"

"It doesn't matter, today's a holiday! You never call anyone 'tu'!"

"I think people in your country call each other 'tu' very freely."

She gave me an indirect smile.

"You understood that, you're pretty smart." She added a few words in her beautiful language. "Do you know this proverb: One calls her 'tu', the other takes her?"

"Am I really a man of the North?"

"Yes, a beautiful face from the North, but you're afraid of the cold."

It's true that I suffered terribly from the cold. When I got back to my corner, again I had a strong desire to drink something. "I'm thirsty," I said. The weather was so dark (so infinitely, uselessly white) I turned my head away so that this hour could do its work. A little after, I called to Claudia: "You should go to sleep." "No," she said. "I'll stay up." I felt very sad. Because the time was approaching, I turned to her again: "Give up this hour. Don't stay. It makes me sad that you're here." But she went on sitting up. Towards five o'clock—when the hour was more advanced—a slight shiver went through me, I opened my eyes for a brief instant, and again, though they were rather far away, I saw certain parts of her face that pierced through the space between us: her prominent cheekbones, her bulging eyes. "Now," I said, "do what you want."

The snow turned into a tempest, the black element of the wind. As I streamed with water, as she dried my face, I heard her call out: "Look: it wasn't a dream! His sweat has soaked my handkerchief." But a little later she lost interest in my "sweat." Surely the day had fruitlessly closed again on the limitlessness of the day. Something had escaped it, its own transparency, that fascinated whiteness that had become the amazement of a cry, a smooth, icy face, frightening and frightened, scattered at random and recaptured at random by the wind.

The cold was affecting her. She drank some tea, no doubt strong and burning, which irritated her throat. When she saw that I was listening to her cough, she went out. Judith came and said to me: "She swallowed the wrong way." "Listen!" I said. "I've heard a sound like that before." She became attentive. "Is it possible," she said, "that...?" But already I no longer wanted to see her or hear her.

Some time must have gone by—the question of how to evaluate time was very different for each of us, even though it was still our time. I will measure its duration very exactly by saying that she only stayed in the hallway long enough to catch her breath, and perhaps she went to drink a mouthful of water. But when she came back, she realized that a much longer period had gone by. She became upset and left the room. When I saw that I was alone I became upset too. Twice I called my brother, but he didn't come. Then I turned back towards that terrifying sound of rumination that now marked time's narrative. But when time speaks, already it is no longer time that is speaking.

While I was still alone (I mean, I had my eyes closed), the bundle of voices loosened, then abruptly came apart. "Quick, a glass of water," I asked. "But you can't drink right now." "Quick, please." Again she said, from very close by, at the level of my mouth: "But you won't be able to swallow." Having suddenly, inordinately, opened my eyes on her after these words, I noticed that her Slavic look (probably because of her fatigue, the late hour) was much more pronounced. "You swallowed the wrong way," I remarked. Apparently I said this in a light, almost playful tone, but I wasn't in the least cheerful. She threatened me with her fist, an image I captured by closing my eyes again. I thought of turning back to myself again, for the third time, but everything at that level appeared to me perfectly tranquil and, in fact, light, almost playful. I rested when I could. I felt rather good. When someone asked me a question, this was what I answered, I or the careless and forgetful echo of time: "Why, it's just fine."

Once again I entered the world of the cheerful life. Yet I can't deny it: whatever sort of tenderness, whatever wonderful kindness emerged from this moment—and perhaps the expression, to be welcomed with open arms, had lost something of its startling truth—the fact that it was "once again" remained difficult to absorb. I think that even for the others something was there that wasn't going by, and I believe that the instant, too, in its joyful sincerity and under its lovely face, became confused by the fact that it had appeared. As for me, I was almost immediately devastated by an extreme feverishness. That idea, "the day is beginning," was burning me, it was already reduced, through my life, to the eternity of so few instants, it was already that other idea, "the day is dying"; haste which was stripped of its composure, like a muddle of actions, and yet was a completely lucid demand, because through its entire extent I saw the immensity of the history that I had to set in motion. I found myself on the same level as this beautiful instant, but could I grasp it? Will anyone have trouble understanding that with its wild strength, the shiver was already dragging me farther along? And what maddened my impatience was that the beautiful instant wanted to be kept, eternalized, it was a cheerful instant that did not know or only suspected that by lingering near me, it was condemning itself to become a beautiful apparition, a return that would be forever beautiful, but separated from itself and from me by the greatest cruelty.

Perhaps this impatience was not apparent to the eyes of the cheerful world; perhaps I seemed at most preoccupied: smiling, but under the veil of preoccupations. At the moment of this awakening, I think the darkest sort of thing was happening. Certainly, I opened my eyes on Claudia and I was already moving towards her with all the impetus of a man who is moving towards the day. But, whether because she was shaken by fatigue or because one can't put up indefinitely with something intolerable, even though she was firm in her resolution, hardly had she touched my look when she uttered an amazing cry, almost a howl, and no doubt she flinched back, but, with a brutality that didn't consider anything, I leaped on her fiercely and seized her again. I won't try to justify this violence. This is how things are. A person who is afraid inspires horror, and a person who weakens becomes the victim of a pitiless and unfair strength.

I must add (to be fair) that I was not certain of this very dark incident, and my uncertainty made it even darker, since it couldn't be brought into the daylight except through a preoccupied "I think." Yet something happened; even though I was once again capable of answering: "Why it's just fine," this answer had an odd ring to it in this cheerful world, and perhaps it wasn't her fault, but I had this impression: by retreating before the facts, she had imprudently drawn into the day a prologue to the day that should never have broached the awakening, a live gleam before which she continued to retreat and which was reflected, it seemed to me, in the menacing expression of her own look, in that fierce yet troubled way she now had of staring at me—fierce, hostile and yet faltering (she had large, bulging eyes, very intense and very dry in their expression; under the veil of preoccupation, they had grown even larger, but had softened, and that softness was menacing). Another sign of her preoccupation was that she tried—when I asked her, but I hadn't let go of her yet: "Have you been here very long?"—to tell me everything or at least to tell me one thing. As far as I could see, it was like a vast landscape of temptation, a prayer for perpetual happiness, an offer to hand me the keys to the kingdom, which finally was illuminated by this expansive sentence (which had every appearance of being an answer to my useless questions about what "exactly" had happened): "No one here wants to be connected to a story."

This sentence made a deep impression on me. I thought I saw light spring from it, I had touched a spot of surprising brightness. A sentence? Something slipping, a portrait not yet framed, a brightly sparkling motion that shone in quick dazzles, and this wasn't a calm light, but a sumptuous and whimsical chance, brightness's mood.

I stayed in the dazzle of that speech. Really, this was a complete restatement, a wonderful summary that seemed to me to throw back into shadow everything that I myself, at certain instants, had been able to conceive of the situation (maybe I should add in my defense that what was happening was simple: I was thinking; more and more ideas were coming to me; who could resist such magic?). And undoubtedly, no matter how much pleasure I took in considering this spectral light, I was not blind to its dangerous aspect, but my look of amazement must have been evident enough so that Claudia thought I had completely entered into that powerful way of seeing. So that when I asked her, pointing to her friend, "And she doesn't either?" she had no difficulty anwering enthusiastically: "She even less than the others!"

I accepted this plain speech as bravely as I could, it had been tossed off so cheerfully (even though "the others" was not the most precise expression); but, in spite of everything, I couldn't share her enthusiasm. Disconcerted, I think I let go of her. But she lost no time catching hold of me again.

"Sometimes she is far away, very far away," she said, making an impressive gesture with her hand.

"In the past?" I asked timidly.

"Oh, much farther away!"

I pondered, trying to discover what could really be farther away than the past. Meanwhile, she seemed all of a sudden afraid that she had thrown me slightly beyond the limits. She squeezed me hard, then she said, hesitantly and in a dejected voice:

"She sees you."

I immediately felt very uneasy. I had to look away from that speech, which was so extraordinarily repugnant (and also contemptuous), and I grew even more uneasy when I heard myself ask her:

"Where?"

"All over, where you are."

I think that as she said that, her voice faltered a little, so that there was a note of tenderness in it that was hardly usual. She allowed my gaze to penetrate hers, which was soft and because of that menacing. Then I noticed how much I liked that menacing gleam, how much it attracted me. I said to her:

"You don't hate me as much as that!"

She pondered this, though she didn't withdraw from my gaze: "I feel a sort of sympathy for you." She leaned towards me and added in her somber voice: "Sympathy for the enemy is a very strong feeling."

"But I'm not your enemy," I said gaily. "I've just woken up and at this moment I'm touching you. I like that very much. Have you been here very long?"

"Be careful," she said, pushing me away and shivering; "She's frail; she's almost no one."

I felt it too, I felt a cold breath, an icy insinuation that seemed to me to come from the awakening (but afterwards I thought the insinuation was deep inside her words, strangely ill situated, because they had seemed to me to concern her, whereas they clearly applied to her friend much more). The confusion was so great that she quickly went back to a less dangerous path and said, with her admirable composure:

"It's natural, you look at what's in front of you. You go as close as possible." Then she added: "Beyond the Urals, you know, in the old days women weren't accustomed to sitting down very often. Even when they didn't have anything left to do, they stood like pillars in their kitchens. At the theater, too, it was normal to stand up."

I didn't manage to approach what she was saying as fast as she was inviting me to. I was waiting for something from the room, I was discovering great sterile spaces in the room that reminded me, actually, of the motionlessness of those vast plains.

"In any case," I said to her, "you're letting yourself get very tired."

"Oh, yes! Very much so." But when I saw the effect of this cry of pleasure, I told her the reasons for it: "It's that you're more approachable," I said to her.

I don't know what she thought of that. She sank into a secret, motionless observation that seemed to be the corollary of everything we had said. But it was soon clear what she was thinking:

"Why aren't you satisfied with what you have?"

I studied her awkwardly.

"But what I have," I said, "I don't have."

Even though what she had said appeared almost inoffensive, it had nevertheless been enough to make a new perspective come up between us. Certainly she wanted to tell me something, but what she also wanted just as much was to make me say something.

"It's pointless for you to stay up," I insisted. "You really have to admit that in spite of everything, it will happen . . ."

"What will happen?"

"Sooner or later all this will slip through your fingers."

If I had counted on this brutal behavior to break down her obstinacy, I was quite wrong.

"Then why," she said, "do you want to do that?"

Why? I laughed at her question.

"But I don't want to," I told her, "I don't want to."

She wasn't very affected.

"Maybe you don't want it in the same way that I can want what I do, but all the same, it's something that is very much wanted: I sense it," she said in a rigid tone of voice.

"Oh, as far as wanting goes, you're very good at that!" I replied agreeably. "Now it's my turn: if 'I want it', why don't you want it?"

But after thinking about it, she betrayed a disturbance, an emotion that surprised me. And she said in her low voice:

"Perhaps I don't want it as much as you think, not as much as before." She stopped for a second. "Sometimes I, too, feel as though I am inside this thing that is wanted."

"You are? Just you?"

"What I want, my will. It doesn't help that I don't let go of anything, that I never lose sight of her—I can't manage it."

Once again her voice had that slight, vibrant faltering that made it so remarkable.

"But it seems to me just the opposite, that so far you've managed it quite well. You've been amazing, you know."

She was hardly listening to me, and yet, through the stream of her thoughts, she really must have discerned the motion of mine, because she alluded to it with an unexpected distress:

"You too, just now, you were so far away . . ."

"I was far away?"

She made an impressive gesture, then, leaning on herself as though to find her balance, she said with a disconsolate tranquillity:

"I don't know if it will last much longer, because this sort of freedom exhausts all one's strength."

I watched her gently for a long time.

"You're a strange woman. So much will, so much courage, such a strong soul, and all that . . . for nothing."

She gave me a terrible look and, as though she were going on with the awakening, threw herself backwards uttering an amazing cry, a real howl.

A short time after, I spoke to her gaily: "Well, that was a terrible fight!" But she gestured to me with her hand. Nevertheless, she caught her breath again and left, doing several things to relax and soothe her throat, which was hardly meant for such vociferations. I emerged from this scene "preoccupied." I had heard her rinsing her throat, performing ablutions, this was a dark noise, the echo of a presentiment so distant that it seemed to come to me across the interstices of time. Was it possible? That she thought she was alive and yet already her mouth was full of fraud? I think she was sleeping, but not very deeply, because as soon as I tried to stand up, she woke up and touched me with her look, this look that stared at things through the menace with which she felt stricken, and this was why it was so menacing. "I hardly believe in you," she said softly. I wasn't surprised by that. It was in keeping with the atmosphere of uncertainty, indecision, and even her sentence was tainted with it, it seems to me; for that reason it was not spiteful, but rather disquieting and even mildly pleasant—an irresponsible and incompetent truth that one didn't want to drive away.

"But... do I want to make something be believed?"

She didn't answer, and while the time passed, I eventually wondered if what I had taken for a speech was not simply a delaying phrase, leaving room for what was essential. This led me to ask her:

"What are you going to say now?"

"I hardly believe in you."

"But..." I said, "why that sentence?"

And it's true that when I saw her stick to this, when I heard her persist in that whispering, but nuanced, voice, which was her voice now—a sort of iridescent sincerity in which there was sadness, cunning and a distant resentment—I found her singularly less innocent, as though the young irresponsible truth had continued to signal to her from a place I couldn't see, and its reflection was what passed between us again, but since this was again, it was no longer inoffensive, nor transparent.

"Believe," I said with a little bitterness, "why do you want to believe? My existence is precarious, is that what you're thinking?"

She stared at me with a doubtful expression, which might have signified a desire to answer and the difficulty of answering, or perhaps fatigue, but also a much more important doubt. I had the distinct feeling that she wasn't inclined to content herself with such weak concessions, and, to tell the truth, when I saw that she wasn't satisfied, I thought she was about to repeat... her sentence, it seemed to me it was already on her lips, I heard it in the emptiness of the air. At that moment my anxiety was so great that, in order to prevent what would have been intolerable to her, to anyone, almost at random—but I knew that by doing this I was yielding infinitely to her, exaggeratedly—I murmured: "You want to say that..." She nodded. "But can it be? Yet you touch me, you speak to me." She straightened up with extraordinary violence. "I'm talking!" she said in a tone of the harshest irony. "I'm talking!" She hurled this word with such incredible harshness that it tore open the whispering and became an ordinary human word, I mean, uttered with her beautiful intact voice. It was so stripped of meaning that I trembled, and the same shiver ran through her. Both of us, it seems to me, were involved in the same fear.

Her reaction had been so strong, she had straightened up with such anger, such complete forgetfulness of the circumstances, that not only had she not let go of me, she had drawn me with her, she had sprung with me into the heart of an element which was truly dangerous, unstable, the element of her irony, her unreal sarcasm, where there was no reward for seriousness. It was in some sense an infinite leap. Even though she was restraining me—and because of that I became aware of my own momentum, my desire to push her in front of me—I couldn't help feeling that the slightest thing could make her fall down. She was holding herself heavily upright, pressed against herself, and all that could be heard was the distinct sound of something opening and closing, a dark movement at the back of her throat, which she was trying to relax. I must have asked her: "Would you like something?" But she practically wrung my hands. It was dark then. It seemed there was nothing more to do but to follow the rise, then the fall, of the spasm, a light bubble that burst gently, so close to me that it was natural for my fate to be linked to that noise. At last she had a slight attack of coughing, which forced her into a silent struggle, because all she could do was suppress completely the vibrations that were passing through her throat, so that she gave the impression of fighting behind closed doors, in a world already far away, to which she had withdrawn out of discretion but also out of mistrust. I think she was very hot. Through this heat she found my hands, which were completely cold. "You're cold as ice," she said. She grasped my two hands and quickly, no doubt in order to enjoy a colder touch, put them flat against her throat.

Now I have to say this: even though I saw how real it was, this gesture left me feeling uncomfortable, uneasy. Why? This is hard to understand, but it made me think of a truth whose shadow it would be, it made me think of some sort of unique, radiant thing, as though it had tried to condemn to mere likeness an inimitable instant. Bitter suspicion, disconcerting and burdensome thought. I remained there in the background as though on the edge of the morning. I asked her—I was half sitting up on the couch, but she was close to the wall, leaning slightly over my hands, which she held firmly against her: "Things should stay this way, shouldn't they?" I think this question went unanswered, because, shortly after, I spoke to her joyfully: "Well, that was a terrible attack!" But when I tried to come even closer, she flinched in a peculiar way. I couldn't help saying: "What's wrong, what's wrong?"—words which I was amazed to hear. I added: "Why are you so nervous?" "Because you look so cheerful." That answer made me laugh and she laughed a little too. A slight motion, but one that overtaxed her dangerously. I felt a terrible, convulsive storm pass between my arms, and in order to stay with her, I had to respond to the awesome appeal that rose from the depths of the day at this instant, I was filled with rage, I seized her around the waist, and now that I had caught hold of her again in the midst of the unsteadiness, the static falling of our two bodies together, I held her firmly out of reach of what had no limit. Little by little, she was able to breathe again, she recovered a slight, individual life, and as I was letting go of her, she murmured something hastily, but to give chaos its revenge, I stopped her from emerging from that instant.

The strange thing about the situation was that I sensed how much she had been telling the truth: she had become upset because I was in good spirits. And suddenly that upset me too. I saw how powerful it was—this cheerful force, this kind of enticing determination, this disturbing will that had forced her to laugh, taken her breath away and made her shiver; it seemed ready to rise, to spring toward the trembling of a much stronger turbulence, no longer a slight, frivolous sparkling, but already a blazing trail and a jubilant wrath and a fiery and furious derision. A storm? But a sterile one, in which the unleashing of the most frivolous lightness would turn into the vertigo of an avid circle, avid to uncoil to infinity. This avidness crossed through the day, tormented space, attracted it, set it in motion and transformed it into a strange blazing wheel without a center; boundless exaltation, depth of bitterness and cruelty, and yet what was it? The frivolity of the most cheerful image. In the past, I had thrown myself toward the cheerful life of the day, an unsituated, elusive event. If I tried to recall to myself that immense plunge, I also had to recall the moment when the brightness had recoiled before me, and it could be that this terrible earlier element which, under cover of this recoil, had risen from the depths of the awakening, was what was tormenting the light day, perhaps its approach was provoking this trembling response, this quick condensation of the brightness into fire, and of the fire into a Yes, Yes, Yes burning around a cold core. Had I plunged? But as I woke up in this life, perhaps I awoke this life with me, and perhaps this jubilation signified some prodigious and terrifying motion, in which two elements soared to meet one another—a frozen day and a burning day, or I who eternally preceded the origin and I who eternally radiated the end.

I can't say I tried to hide from this motion. I couldn't have, I didn't want to. But it's true that I also wanted to go back to something serious, I couldn't do without what really has to be called a serious truth. At this instant, Claudia seemed like a true affirmation, an extraordinarily opulent affirmation. I think I hadn't imagined that she would still have so much strength, as though no part of her life was at all worn, though I saw her passing through it. I thought: "Why, she is extraordinarily lonely," and I thought she was lonely because she hadn't vanished, along with everything else, into the illusion of a memoryless intimacy. In a sense this was disconcerting. I asked her: "Do you need air?" "Do you?" Her voice seemed more veiled to me than I had expected, she wasn't weak, she still had a sort of fullness, authority, that I imagine she derived from the force of the way she had spoken. "Does it make you tired to talk?" "No, not at this moment, not with you." I still hadn't let go of her, I held her with all the energy the surprise of her own strength had given me. "Well," I said to her joyfully, "talk to me." "Just like that? Talk nonsense? Without stopping?" I noticed that she had turned toward me, and yet not completely; really, as I listened to her I experienced an extraordinary pleasure, because it was so distinct, so full, though under the veil of a whisper. This was why I was induced to answer: "But you have a lot to say to me now." "To you?" "To me," I said gaily, "to me." Yet I felt her withdraw, contract, and I leaned my head forward: "I think a little noise..." This seemed to tempt her. "Noise?" I nodded. We stayed that way, both of us, waiting.

I think she slept, but not very deeply, because as soon as I stood up she was standing up too. I asked her where Judith was. "Who is Judith?" "Your friend. That's the name I gave her." "I don't like that name. She went to bed. She needs her sleep too." "You leave her alone?" As I was going toward the window, she tried to help me walk. "I'm not a drunk." It was raining now, a peaceful rain that signalled the slow decline of winter. I asked her to point out the different streets to me, and she did: Trinité, Boulevard Haussman, Passage de la Bourse. "Do you like this city?" No, she didn't like it. "Does it make you tired to talk?" "A little." "Was it singing that hurt your throat?" "Singing was what started it. People who sing have to expect problems like that." "I don't know if I told you this, I don't like singing very much, but listening to you was a pleasure." She went to look for her mechanical pencil, which I think she used for writing when she couldn't speak, then slowly she came back and sat down on the couch, and because I was near the window I could see how much lighter, how much larger the room had grown. I looked at the immense space, the wall over there, the door farther off, a little closer the depth of a blank spot. I said to her: "Come to the South with me." She shook her head. "It isn't possible." "Come!" She helped me to take a few steps, at first with rather bad grace, then with a tentative good will. When we reached the middle of the room, she left me, opened the door and went into the hall. It was very dark there, but since she was walking just a little ahead of me, I could distinguish her very clearly. As soon as I appeared, she started walking again; she moved off slowly, with a great and melancholy dignity, turning back slightly to see if she was being followed, but still not stopping. At the point where the hall bent, she paused (I had to adjust to the different air); when the gap between us was small enough, she moved away from the wall and plunged into the even darker part that led to the vestibule. Now I found myself at the point where the hall forked. I stayed there a little while. But when the bedroom door opened, I went on too.

Her friend looked at us both, one after the other, I think, and even though she had turned her head slightly in my direction, something incredibly piercing in this look, coming together with the lively movement of her eyes, immobilized us. I don't think

I've ever seen a look as avid as that one. Feelings can be read in the eyes—terror, the shock of desire—but this look was avid, I mean it didn't express light: not clear, not cloudy, and really, perhaps because of its fixity, which was made even more provoking by the fact that her eyes darted back and forth (looking at each of us in turn), if it expressed anything it was the shamelessness of hunger, the nocturnal surprise before the prey. It was certainly a wonderful look: avid? but possessing nothing, insignificant but capable of an immense sarcasm—and more than anything, very beautiful.

She didn't seem dazed, as she would have been if she had just woken up, because when Claudia roughly pulled the covers off her she simply watched with the same expression of sarcastic avidness—and now this avidness was also, it seems to me, curiously interested—but without any surprise. This action didn't bother her, in any case; slyly, she too contemplated her nocturnal body, this body that had been tumbled over into the night. She had her arms modestly down by her sides, in the age-old attitude of repose (but her hand was tightly clenched). Then Claudia did this: she touched her arm to raise it (or shift it), and when it didn't yield, she tried to open her hand. What followed was the work of an instant: with amazing spirit, Judith sat up, shouted two words—then sank back on the bed.

A terrible scene, but one that left me with a feeling of joy, of limitless pleasure. That wonderful head that had been uplifted, what could be more true, and if it had then been thrown down lower than the earth, that was just as much part of the exaltation, that was proof of it, the moment when one no longer worshipped the majesty of a piece of debris, but seized it and tore it apart.

I think the vitality of that scene was all the more overwhelming because it was contained in two or three gestures. What had been depicted was inscribed on an infinitely thin film, but behind it rumbled the freedom of a pure caprice in which the taste for blood hadn't yet been awakened. No one could say of such a scene that it had ever taken place before; it had occurred a first time and only once and its exuberance was the enrgy of the origin, from which nothing springs. Even when I went back over it to "think" about it—and it required that: an intense meditation—it didn't take me anywhere; face to face we held each other, not at a distance, but in the intimacy of a mysterious familiarity, because she was "you" for me, and I was "me" for her.

What could I have said about it? She wasn't for one moment unforgettable, she didn't want to be held sacred: even when she was terrifying, there was something extraordinarily cheerful about her. No doubt this could not be relived, the moment of collapse, the dreadful alteration of life, unable to control itself, was a blow to memory—and afterwards? afterwards, chaos and yet I swear the last instant infinitely surpassed all the others, because it was on me that this dream body had decomposed, I had held it in my arms, I had experienced its strength, the strength of a dream, of a desperate gentleness, defeated and still persevering, such as only a creature with avid eyes could communicate it to me.

I would like to say this: when a man has lived through something unforgettable, he shuts himself up with it to grieve over it, or he sets off to find it again; he thus becomes the ghost of the event. But this face did not concern itself with memory, it was fixed but unstable. Had it happened once? A first time and yet not the first. It had the strangest relations with time, and this was uplifting too: it did not belong to the past, a face and the promise of that face. In some way it had looked at itself and seized itself in one single instant, after which this terrifying contact had occurred, this mad catastrophe, which could certainly be considered its fall into time, but that fall had also crossed time and carved out an immense emptiness, and this pit appeared to be the jubilant celebration of the future: a future that would never again be new, just as the past refused to have taken place once.

Claudia came back shortly after I did. I could add that these words, which, in my eyes, had once ushered in Claudia's life and made her the person who comes after, came back too, and drew me toward the same truth: I didn't know her. In this way, the whole cycle began again. But though I was still deep inside this intense meditation, I could certainly see her coming near, coming from the depths of return, slowly, with her great and melancholy dignity, I could see her pass close to me and, close though she was, stare at me for a brief instant beyond boundary after boundary, and all this had the dark power of "I didn't know her," but all this also signified the exaltation of this return, the fact that it was a monumental event, elevated to its own glory, in a light that proclaimed not an absent and motionless truth, but the blaze of an ultimate meaning. Yes, she came back shortly afterwards and I didn't know her. But no longer in the light of those feeble words, for they had been obliterated, swept away by the terrifying breath of the two words howled by Judith from the depths of her memory, *Nescio vos*, "I don't know who you are," which she had thrown in our faces, and afterwards she had sunk back in my arms.

The greatest and truest utterance, for me, the radiant heart, the expression of the familiarity and the jealousy of night. And it is true that even these words, these words too, were an echo of another time, she had to have learned them from someone (she was ignorant of almost everything), but what I had perhaps let fall as a grammatical fact was being thrown back at me by the immensity, after great labor on the part of the shadows, thrown back into my face as the benediction and malediction of the night.

Claudia came back shortly after I did. Everything was quiet, and I think she rested then. And yet, later, I saw *her* looking at me through the open door of the hall (I was opposite, in the studio). When I saw her again, she was sitting down, and across the whole space she appeared slightly lower than I was, her body half inclined, her head bent towards her knees. It had happened to me in the past, when I lived alone in the South—and I was in the prime of life, during the day my strength was staggering; but there was a moment in the night when everything would stop—hope, possibility, and the night; then I would open the door and I would look tranquilly down at the bottom of the stairway: it was a completely tranquil and intentionless movement, purely nocturnal, as they say. At this instant, across the immense space, she gave me the impression that she too was sitting down at the bottom of a stairway, on the large step where the stairs turn; having opened the door, I looked at her, she was not looking at me, and all the tranquillity of this movement, which was so perfectly silent, today had the truth of this body slightly stooped in an attitude that was not one of expectation, nor of resignation, but of a profound and melancholy dignity. For my part, I could do no more than look at this woman with a gaze that expressed all the calm transparency of a last gaze, as she sat near the wall, her head leaning slightly towards her hands. Could I approach her? Could I go down? I didn't want to, and she herself, in her unwarranted presence, was accepting my look, but not asking for it. She never turned towards me and after I had looked at her I never forgot to go away calmly. This instant was never disturbed, or prolonged, or deferred, and maybe she didn't know me, and maybe she was unknown to me, but it didn't matter, because for one and for the other this instant really was the awaited moment, for both of us the time had come.

Now I have to say it: when the face of such a moment shows

itself, one mustn't respect it (bind oneself to it by the sense of something amazing). Certainly, it is a supreme apparition, but this supremacy is that of someone who wants to be not only seen but touched—and not only respected but loved—and not feared at all, because terror would become its temptation, and whoever closes his eyes in its presence makes it blind, just as he who respects it encloses it in the futility of a cold and unreal life. When, in the past, in the South, I shut the door again, I knew that this door represented the proud decision that made it possible for distress to manifest itself to me with such extraordinary dignity, to live near me and for me to live near it, and I knew that that instant would have been turned into humiliation and shame, if I had tried to perpetuate it or tried to find it again. During the day, I didn't think about it; and yet, in the midst of this unconcern, there was no day for me except through the strength of my relationship to this single unknown point and through the even more unknown relationship of this point to me: if this relationship was threatened (but what did the word threatened mean, in such a situation? It really had no meaning, that's why I didn't think about it), the day was also jeopardized and the unconcern turned into an irresolute "I don't remember any more" transmitted to one another by every thing and every hour. In any case, this relationship did not make daily life easy. I did not lack strength, and certainly, when the day began, my understanding with this beginning was an understanding with youth, an understanding on the part of what makes a decision and from the outset goes beyond it. I was leading a more or less normal life; I was in good health, as they say; now and then I wrote a few words—these words, to be precise—but what "exactly" was happening? I wouldn't be able to say, beyond making this observation: that even though I wasn't thinking about it at all, I had bound myself to this "point" and I was looking at it with such self-abuse that the strength of even a more capable man probably wouldn't have been enough for it and that in any case mine, the strength of the day, of the day that was mine, was no longer equal to the tasks of daily life, even though, I must confess, this life was often reduced to very little.

But was this really true and was I looking? Not at something, not at a point, not at anything. I would have been horrified at myself if, on the occasion of that image, which was so discreet, I had shown any interest in it or paid any attention to it. Understand, it was in no way a matter of an image: the image or the figure, however quiet, was, in relation to the supreme dignity of the instant, no more than a vestige of uneasiness, the uneasiness remained poised on the instant, that was why it became apparent. What I mean is that the day evidently had a relationship with that instant of the night, a mysterious, dramatic, and in every way exhausting relationship, and since I too loved the day and since I was also alive, I was involved in the most exhausting intrigue, but that still didn't mean that I was really occupied by it.

I burned, but this terrible fire was the shudder of the distance, and no task corresponded to that distance. I grew more silent (and since I was alone, that meant silent towards myself). Extraordinarily idle and yet having little time. To some degree, my life was exuberance, but to some degree it was poverty of breath, and I could no doubt say to myself that because the forces of desire had bound themselves, in me, to the truth of a single instant, I really had to give that truth not only myself, not only everything, but even more (and more, I imagine, meant the scald of being, which eternally denies the end), but such a calming explanation did not explain to me why I was this torch lit in order to illuminate a single instant, and when one burns with impatience, explaining is the sort of baseness never permitted by the day, though it is in the day that the shudder comes to light. Things happened to me, to me and to the story, events that were more and more curtailed (in the sense that, just as I had become no one or almost no one as the traits of my character weakened, the world was also readily merging with its limit), but this sort of penury of time was disclosing above all the exorbitant pressure of "Something is happening," a jealous immensity that could only curtail or suspend the natural progress of the story. The reason for the strangeness was this: that this extraordinary, living pressure was not that of a point foreign to time, but represented as well the pure passion of time, the pure power of the day, and its exigency did not turn away from life but rather consumed it the moment it touched it and appeared unlivable, in exactly the same way that passion is living, even though the creature touched by passion also destroys the possibility that is life. That is why, in certain respects, this "point" was passion in this world, and the passion of the world could only seek this point.

It could be that I lived in the state of anxiety of a man obliged to take upon himself the anxiety and work of the day —a day that had not begun and was not yet shining except in the distant beginning of an image whose calm was distress and whose supremacy was origin and end. At night, when I got up, who got up with me? At that instant, there was no day, no night, no possibility, no expectation, no uneasiness, no repose, but nevertheless a man standing wrapped in the silence of this speech: there is no day and yet it is day, so that this woman sitting down there against the wall, her body half inclined, her head bent toward her knees, was no closer to me than I was near her, and the fact that she was there did not mean that she was there, nor I, but the conflagration of this speech: now it is happening, something is happening, the end is beginning.

When I opened the door, no one would ask me where I was going: there was no one to ask me. When I returned, no one asked me where I had been. Now, someone is asking me: "Why, when did you go out?" "Just now."

It is true that I'm talking about anxiety, but it is the shiver of joy that I'm talking about—and distress, but the luster of this distress. I may appear to be prey to the limitless torment of an exorbitant constraint that is also incomprehensible, to the point where if I say, if I too say, the day is night for me, I will express something of this torment. And yet, a mild torment, for in front of me is the lightning, behind me the fall, and in me the intimacy of the shock.

I met this woman I called Judith: she was not bound to me by a relationship of friendship or enmity, happiness or distress; she was not a disembodied instant, she was alive. And yet, as far as I can understand, something happened to her that resembled the story of Abraham. When Abraham came back from the country of Moria, he was not accompanied by his child but by the image of a ram, and it was with a ram that he had to live from then on. Others saw the son in Isaac, because they didn't know what had happened on the mountain, but he saw the ram in his son, because he had made a ram for himself out of his child. A devastating story. I think Judith had gone to the mountain, but freely. No one was freer than she was, no one troubled herself less about powers and was less involved with the justified world. She could have said, "It was a God who wanted it," but for her that amounted to saying, "It was I alone who did it." An order? Desire transfixes all orders.

It wasn't true that we understood each other: on the contrary, there was no understanding. She was, in a sense, much more visible than I, and the more time passed, the more the day and the luster of the day allowed her to be seen, but the hour also came when the blazing frontiers had been crossed and to look at her was to deny almost everything. Unstable? She was not less so than I was. And jealous? Certainly. Capable of violence, even a storm; space fled before her. She had bound herself furiously to the infinite; only there could she find a language in which to say, "Even so, I see it!" But the limitless was not enough for her. That was why she was eternally summoning me out of the infinite.

The fact that she was more and more obvious—this was her splendor, a threat directed against herself—proclaimed that she was alive: yes, she was taking flight, the companion of a single moment. And now? Now, the obviousness had been shattered; the broken pillars of time were holding up their own ruins.

"Now"—strange ray. Now—furious force, pure truth deprived of counsel. It was quite true that we understood each other, but in the depth of now, where passion means loving and not being loved. One who loves is the magnificence of the end; one who is loved is miserly care, obedience to the end. She was bound to me because she radiated the joyful power in whose light I loomed up precisely here, precisely now—at her touch—and I was bound to her because I was the day that made me touch her obviousness. But if "this relationship was threatened," she became a sterile "I want it" and I became a cold and distant image.

She had looked at me for a long time, but I did not see her. Days that were supreme in her eyes. That she was in this way unknown was not a misfortune for her; and her gaze was not modest, but avid: as I said, the most avid of all, since it had nothing. Yet she yielded to the shudder; she stared at me from the depths of an extreme past, a wild place, towards an extreme future, a desert place, and because she was not at all contemplative, that look, oddly brazen, was a constant, violent attempt to seize me, a drunken, joyful challenge unconcerned about either possibility or the moment. Because of that, she was ahead of me, and yet her youth had something unreal about it, a prophetic transparency that injured time and made it anxious about itself. Subjugate me? She didn't want that. Let herself be guided? She couldn't. Touch me? Yes; it was this contact that she called the world, world of a single instant, an instant before which time rebels.

So I remained alone, I mean that I went away, then, into the depths, because in order for her to become visible too, no doubt she had to stop seeing me. Hunger, cold—she lived among such elements, but starved as she was, she moved off as soon as her gaze risked awakening mine, and not with the timidity of a weak soul, but because wildness was her dominion. Without a wild movement, what chance would she have had of springing towards me? But to allow her that leap, I too must draw back and draw back again.

At night, in the South, when I get up, I know that it isn't a question of proximity, or of distance, or of an event belonging to me, or of a truth capable of speaking, this is not a scene, or the beginning of something. An image, but a futile one, an instant, but a sterile one, someone for whom I am nothing and who is nothing to me—without bonds, without beginning, without end—a point, and outside this point, nothing, in the world, that is not foreign to me. A face? But one deprived of a name, without a biography, one that is rejected by memory, that does not want to be recounted, that does not want to survive; present, but she is not there; absent, and yet in no way elsewhere, here; true? altogether outside of what is true. If someone says, she is bound to the night, I deny it; the night doesn't know her. If someone asks me, but what are you talking about? I answer, well, there is no one to ask me that. And the day? The day asks nothing of her, it is not involved with her, it owes her neither loyalty nor belief. I myself haven't looked for her, I haven't questioned her, and if I pass near there, I don't stop. What sort of relations do we have? I don't know. Yet I can sense that the day is bound to her in some way. That there is, between them, not an understanding but the envelopment of a mutual temptation, the rustle of reciprocal

67

attractions—this is no doubt what appears when the day, idle in the midst of its tasks, seems to play with a frivolous power that makes it lighter and freer. I can say that I have witnessed this game, if it is a game. But if it is madness, I can see that I participate in it.

I don't think I've ever been unaware of it, I know I'm mixed up in a profound, static intrigue, one that I mustn't look at, or even notice, that I mustn't be occupied by and that nevertheless requires all my strength and all my time. I will say it again, there is no room around me for an anomaly. The anomaly would be diversion reduced to limits, perceptible and pacifying, though disquieting. But diversion is restless, it doesn't stop anywhere. It doesn't appear at one spot or another, it only causes appearances to be brighter, more evident and also more extensive, so that the boundaries themselves have the beautiful tranquillity of the surface. A tranquillity that is difficult to contain and, I'm convinced, very strange, even though nothing mysterious or reserved is hidden in it; on the contrary, what it portends is that the day is giving up its profound reserve. The day is without depth, I mean without reserve of future, without a bond with the day, it is untrammeled brightness, transparency extolling itself, a festival, a floating festival, a game in which haste, torment, and agitation are lost—and also definite calm and repose.

Maybe this movement was imperceptible, I don't know. I never saw anything in myself or outside myself that marked any change whatsoever. It's true that when there isn't any air, at a certain moment time becomes the air that breathing exhausts. But if my breath doesn't have any time, this isn't because time is limited, for it doesn't seem to have any limits any more, it is only more attenuated and poorer, and because of that unstable and fleeting. I think I can no longer lose my time, and for a peculiar reason, really, which is that it has already lost itself, having fallen below the things one can lose, having become unknowable, alien to the category of lost time. A mysterious impression, since I occupy myself with fewer and fewer things and yet I am always entirely occupied. What is more, I am subjected to a constant, extreme pressure to reduce my tasks even further, though they are already so far reduced. Surprising, instantaneous obviousness.

I think that time goes by, because after all the days go by, slip past, and with a joyful promptness in the heart of their tranquil light. But I see clearly that for me there is only less and less time at the instant where I am, which explains not why nothing happens, but why what happens is like the repetition of one and the same event—and yet not the same: it sinks to a lower and lower level, where it seems to wander rather in the manner of an image, even though it is absolutely present.

I spoke of an intrigue. It is true that this word is intended to fill a hopeless function, but even so, it expresses in its own way the feeling I have: that I am bound, not to a story, but to the fact that, as I am likely to have less and less of a story, this poverty, far from winning me simpler days, attracts what life I have left in a cruelly complex movement of which I know nothing, if not that it excites the impatience of a desire that doesn't want to wait any longer, as though I were supposed to make my way as soon as possible to the place it is urging me to come to, even though it consists precisely in distancing me from every end and forbidding me to go anywhere.

Anyone who wants to live has to rely on the illusion of a story, but this reliance is not permitted to me. I must recall this: such days are not devoted to an unknown misfortune, they don't confirm the distress of a moribund decision; on the contrary, they are traversed by joyful immensity, a radiant authority, luminescence, pure frivolity, too strong for the days, turning them into a pure dissipation and each event into the image of a displaced episode (an episode that is not in its place, a sort of farce of time, belonging to a different age, a lost and baffled fragment of history). I sometimes think: "I believe I'm going to suffocate from such a lack of memory," but forgetfulness has in no way passed over things. On the contrary, recollection is the ponderous form of this lack of memory. A terrible pause in which nothing stops. It may be that where I am, I have too much of a sort of courage (a sort of dread). This courage keeps me on my feet. I am not unaware that what I have searched for is searching for me at this hour. What I have looked at wants to look me in the face. But to remain on one's feet—how can one give that up? This will is mysterious. I also have the feeling that I am not only staying in my place—yes, with a certain absurd obstinacy, in my place, on my feet—but even more: I have become a little unstable, I move from spot to spot. Of course I don't take many steps, but when I go by, doors slam, the light air runs across the space. Anyone who meets me thinks, "So he is there, at present," but, immediately, "Oh! But here, now!" Is it night? The morning burns. I go down the stairs; again there is emptiness, the gaity of emptiness, the joyful shiver of space and no one, really, is there to notice it; it is true that I myself undoubtedly know something about this light and furtive thrust, about this roving air that hardly disturbs the expanse and that leads me here, and here, but it doesn't seem to concern me particularly; this is how the day is, an endless shimmer, footsteps wandering through the rooms, the muffled thumps of work.

Forgetfulness has not passed over things, but I must say this: that in the brightness where they glitter, in this brightness that doesn't destroy their limits, but unites the unlimited with a constant and joyful "I see you," they shine in the intimacy of a new beginning in which nothing else has a place; and as for me, through them I have the immobility and inconstancy of a reflection, an image wandering among images and drawn along with them in the monotony of a movement that appears to have no conclusion just as it had no beginning. Perhaps, when I get up, I have faith in the beginning: who would rise if he didn't know the day was beginning? But, even though I am still capable of taking many steps, which is why doors slam, windows open and, the light coming in once again, all things are also in their places, unalterable, joyful, definitely present, with a presence that is firm and even so definite and so constant that I know they are indelible, immobile in the glittering eternity of their images. But, seeing them there, where they are, slightly distanced from themselves within their presence, and transformed, by this imperceptible withdrawal, into the happy beauty of a reflection, even though I am still capable of taking many steps, I too can do no more than come and go in the tranquil immobility of my own image, bound to the floating festival of an instant that no longer passes. It may seem astonishing that I should descend so far from myself, into a place one could, I think, call the abyss, and that it should only have surrendered me to the joyful space of a festival, the eternal glitter of an image, and I would be surprised by this too, if I had not felt the burden of this indefatigable lightness, the infinite weight of a sky in which what one sees remains there, where the boundaries sprawl out and the distance shines night and day with the radiance of a beautiful surface.

How terrible things are, when they come out of themselves, into a resemblance in which they have neither the time to corrupt themselves nor the origin to find themselves and where, eternally their own likenesses, they do not affirm themselves but rather, beyond the dark flux and reflux of repetition, affirm the absolute power of this resemblance, which is no one's and which has no name and no face. That is why it is terrible to love and we can love only what is most terrible. To bind oneself to a reflection—who would consent to that? But to bind oneself to what has no name and no face and to give that endless, wandering resemblance the depth of a mortal instant, to lock oneself up with it and thrust it along with oneself to the place where all resemblance yields and is shattered—that is what passion wants. I can say that I bound myself to the immobility that passes both through the night and through the day, the calm phosphorescence of an instant that does not know the eclipse of shadows, that is not extinguished, does not illuminate, for it reveals nothing, is the sparkling happiness of a ray, but this immobility also wanders everywhere, and perhaps I would better tolerate an obviousness that I would never have a hope of seeing elsewhere, a monumental column before which one would remain standing, but this perpetual movement, this infinite caprice, this pursuit that leaves me in the same place and yet makes me keep changing place leads me to believe in a true movement, a movement that is alive and seeks life, even if it is enveloped in the power and the immobility of destiny. Each day, or at least certain days, but also each period of time and each movement of the day shows rne, through the radiant space, the flight of a free image soaring from a point that I can't see toward another point that I can't see, and for me both no doubt merge, it is a fixed ascension, full of splendor, but also a dark effort, a cold fantasy, always the same and always futile, out of which likeness comes to affirm likeness, without this amazing activity being able to do anything more than give me the strength to follow the image instant by instant, an image myself, projected into the fire of appearances, as if, in expressing ourselves through each other, both of us were pursuing the possibility of giving an empty point the luster and the living value of a real meaning. And certainly, the point remains empty, in the same way that even though this can keep beginning again, the beginning always remains silent and unknown, but—and this is the strange thing—I don't worry about it and I go on seizing the instant again with an incredible avidity, the same instant through which I seem to catch sight of this glimmer: someone is there who is not speaking, who is not looking at me, yet who is capable of an entrancing life and cheerfulness, though that cheerfulness is also the echo of a supreme event reverberating through the infinite lightness of time, where it cannot settle.

I can't say I'm always conscious of it, of this glimmer, I would probably have to recognize that it often leaves me free, but, how shall I put it, this glimmer is freedom in me, a freedom that tears apart all bonds, that abolishes all tasks, that allows me to live in the world, but on condition that I am almost no one there, and if I have actually seen myself reduced to the transparency of a being one doesn't encounter, this is because little by little it has relieved me of myself, of my character, of the serious and active affirmation that my character represented. What am I, for it? Someone living in the world? With whom it agrees? A face? But it can't dwell in the world, and I know—in the depths of an ignorance, I admit, that can't take this into consideration—that it has the strength of a single instant, that it knows me but doesn't recognize me, that it touches me, and the future is not bound to it but unbound from it. A face? Where it sees me there may be a face, but enveloped, enclosed in the eternity of a reflection, if it is true that the shadow of things is the shining resemblance into which they withdraw and which throws them back infinitely from likeness to likeness.

I think that this is the absolutely dark moment of the plot, the point at which it keeps returning to the present, at which I can no longer either forget or remember, at which human events, around a center as unstable and immobile as myself, indefinitely construct their return. I can recall which road I was made to take by this and how I broke with almost everything—and in this sense too I have forgotten everything—why, as far away as I am, I have to draw back and draw back again into the heart of the instant where I wander like an image bound to a day that passes immobile through the day and to a time that at a certain point always disengages itself from time. I can recall that, however long this road may be and whatever may be its detours through the futile repetition of days and of moments, nothing can prevent it from being once again and yet again the hallway that separated the two small rooms and that I happened to enter: a vacillating darkness where I had to endure the greatest pain and yet came upon the truest and most joyful moment, as though what I had stumbled against was not the cold truth, but the truth transformed into the violence and the passion of the end. I can recall all that, and to recall it is no doubt only one more step into that same space, where to go farther is already to bind myself to the return. And yet, even though the circle is already drawing me along, and even if I had to write this eternally, I would write it in order to obliterate eternity: Now, the end.